DON'T LOOK NOW -

The Smart Slant On Misdirection

By Al Leech

We pride ourselves on finding people in magic who seem to know some of the answers, and getting them to put their ideas on paper. Such a find is AL LEECH - a man who is in a position to analyze human actions.

Mr. Leech is a United Press news reporter, a job that has taught him a great deal about human nature. His avocation is magic, and in doing his magic he applies what he has learned about psychology in his regular job. His discussions on the psychology of magic, misdirection, how best to fool people, how to make them like you, etc. etc. interested us so much that we urged him to write it down for you.

It is now ready - in a concise little book at a fair little price —

DON'T LOOK NOW! The really smart slant on misdirection in magic.

Find out what makes magic "go". Add the "smart slant" to what you already know about magic and see the difference!

ORDER YOUR COPY TODAY.   . . . .

$ 2.00

FOR CARD MEN ONLY   By Al Leech

Author Leech has made a valiant effort to get away from the too familiar "take a card".

Contents:

Printed, Howatt illustrated.

MIRACLE COIN ACT

Here is an easy trick that requires no skill but has the appearance of highly skillful manipulation. First an empty glass is shown and covered with a silk. Four real half dollars are placed on a handsome wooden coin stand, as seen in the illustration. Performer picks up one coin at a time, tosses it into the air and it vanishes. This is repeated until all the coins have vanished. As each coin is tossed into the air, it is HEARD to enter the glass. When the silk is removed from the "empty" glass, THE FOUR COINS ARE POURED OUT. Truly a miracle! Price includes coin stand, glass and complete routine . . . only.. **$8.50**

COIN THROUGH MATCH

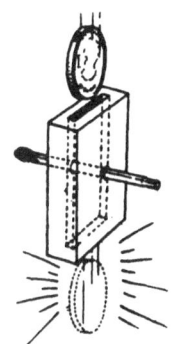

Just the trick for that impromptu call. A coin slide, just large enough to allow a penny to slide through is freely shown. A borrowed match is pushed through a hole in the tube, crosswise, which bars the penny from sliding through. The performer does the impossible, the penny apparently falls through the tube past the match bar.

The borrowed match extends clear through the tube; and is returned unharmed. A truly startling trick.

Simple to do, after you know the secret, but just let someone try who doesn't know. Price............... **$1.00**

PENNY BALANCER

This trick seems almost impossible, but you can do it immediately, with the aid of a secret "gimmick": Here's the effect: You balance one penny on the upright edge of another, as seen in the first illustration.
You then TWIST the penny so it is now crosswise to the other coin and still continue to balance both coins as shown in the second illustration. Both pennies are now given for examination. Others trying to balance the coins FAIL. You can do it again and again. This trick makes a JUGGLER of you in one lesson! Note: Your hands are shown EMPTY at conclusion of trick. $1.50

PRESTO COIN VANISH

A splendid trick that looks like sleight of hand but is easy to do. Performer places a half dollar size coin on his leg, and covers it with a fold of the trousers. When the fold is opened, presto, the coin has vanished! Performer then reproduces the coin from his pocket and offers it for examination $1.00

D. ROBBINS & CO., Inc.

127 W. 17th Street   **New York 11, N. Y.**

Magicians—ORDER these items from your nearest E-Z Magic Dealer. Order directly from us if no dealer is conveniently located.

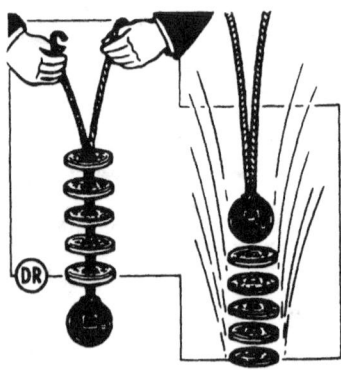

ORIENTAL COIN MYSTERY

This clever pocket trick is a real baffler! You show 5 WHITE Chinese coins threaded on a string, and a RED coin is threaded at the bottom of the string. A spectator holds both ends of the string. It seems IMPOSSIBLE for the WHITE coins to escape . . . yet that is exactly what happens! At conclusion, spectator is still holding ends of string, with red coin threaded, and the white coins are FREE. Easy to do! **$1.00**

NO SLEIGHT COIN ACT

The coins supplied with this trick will enable any amateur magician to make his audience believe that he is a sleight of hand expert. NO SKILL REQUIRED! Here are a few of the effects: After both hands are shown empty, a coin suddenly appears at the tip of fingers. The coin is waved in the air, vanishes, and then is found in a pocket previously shown to be empty. Coin held at finger-tips suddenly becomes TWO coins. Coins and illustrated instructions furnished. **$1.00**

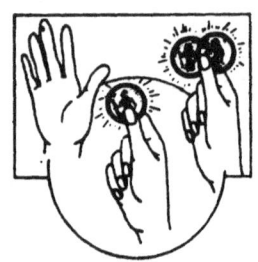

SIMPLEX MISER'S DREAM

This is an easy method for doing the highly popular Miser's Dream effect, with a borrowed drinking glass. Both hands can be shown absolutely empty at the start and finish of the trick, yet almost immediately you can start producing real half dollars "out of the air." Each coin is visibly thrown into the glass . . . the audience SEES IT and HEARS it! Yet you continue to "catch" other coins from your ear, your nose, from a spectator's mouth, etc.

The secret gimmicks supplied for this trick are different from those furnished for our "Coins From the Air" trick. A clearly written routine included with the gimmicks. —————————————— **$2.00**

MANIPULATING WITH LEECH

by

Al Leech

-
-
-
-
-
-
-
-

Published by

MAGIC, INC. Chicago, Ill.

First printing, 1952
Second printing, 1975

STOP LIGHT THIMBLES

Here is a thimble quickie which can be used by itself as an impromptu effect or as part of a longer routine.

As the spectators see it, a red thimble is placed in the left fist and a green one in the pocket. The green one changes to red, and the fist is shown to contain a yellow thimble.

Beforehand, place a red thimble on the right forefinger, a green one on the second finger and a yellow one on the third. Bend the third and little fingers into the palm, concealing the yellow thimble.

Stand facing the audience and begin the effect by showing the red and green thimbles. Tell the audience they represent stop lights and that you are going to conduct a driver's test. Hold the left hand with its palm facing the audience, fingers pointing toward the floor. Place the red and green thimbles against the palm.

Turn the left hand inward toward yourself, at the same time extending the third finger and removing the yellow thimble with the left hand, which closes into a loose fist. Figure 1 shows this

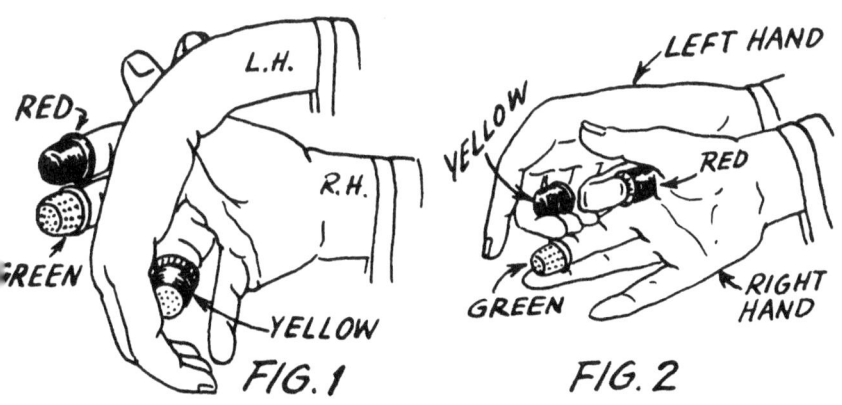

FIG. 1   FIG. 2

steal from the performer's viewpoint. When the steal is complete and the yellow thimble secured in a finger palm position in the crook of the left third finger, hold the red and green thimbles against the back of the left fist for a moment as if for emphasis.

Next, pretend to remove the red thimble with the left hand,

3.

thumb palming it instead in the right hand in the familiar man- ner. To execute this move, simply bring the left hand in front of the right first finger, opening the fist slightly but maintaining the grip on the yellow thimble. As soon as the left hand covers the right forefinger, bend this finger into the thumb crotch and palm the thimble, figure 2. Then, straighten the forefinger and pretend to remove the thimble by pulling it off in the left hand.

Show the green thimble remaining on the right second finger and announce that you will put it in your pocket. Place the right hand in the right trouser pocket and with the tips of the first and third fingers, push the green thimble from the second fingertip, letting it fall into the pocket.

Get the red thimble on the tip of the first finger and remove the hand from the pocket to show that the green thimble has changed to red. Patter to the effect that the stop light changed. Remark that the green thimble must be in the left hand. Show the right hand clean, and push the right second finger into the left fist. Remove the yellow thimble on its tip, pattering that the green light has changed to yellow.

- - - - - - - - -

MULTIPLYING THIMBLES.

This is the classic of thimble magic, but many performers have been dissuaded from attempting the feat because of the difficul- ties involved in stealing the thimbles.

The trouble seems to lie with the various types of thimble hold- ers designed and offered to the magical fraternity. Some of these do not hold the thimbles securely. Others are made of metal and talk. Sponge rubber has been used and it does kill the clatter. But virtually all the holders on the market are awkward to use because they do not conform to the shape of the hand.

After investing a small fortune in thimble holders and experi- menting with numerous designs of my own, I finally made one which I have used for years without a hitch.

It's a homemade item which anyone can assemble. Go to the dime store and buy a pair of the blue and white gloves worn by workmen. Get them a couple of sizes too large. Unless you want to perform a rather elaborate routine, you will need only one glove, but Woolworth's will insist that you buy both of them.

With a pair of scissors cut the left glove in half, cutting cross- wise across the palm, just below the thumb. Throw the thumb

4.

and wrist portion away. To prevent the raw edge from raveling roll it downward on the outside and stitch all the way around it with a needle and coarse thread.

Obtain some stiff felt and cut out a piece just large enough to fit inside your inner breast pocket of your coat. Place the back of the glove lengthwise against the felt. Stitch the back of each finger to the felt, stitching the finger its entire length. This completes the holder, and all that remains is to pin it in place.

It is not essential that you pin the holder inside the pocket, but this procedure has its advantages. In case you want to pull back your coat in some other trick, you will not inadvertently expose the holder if it is in the pocket. At any rate, pin the holder inside the coat on the right side. Use straight pins, one at each corner of the felt.

If you pin the holder inside the pocket, pin it so that the pocket will not turn inside out when you steal the thimbles from the glove. Always test the holder to see that it is pinned properly before performing. Once it is in place, all that remains is to insert a thimble in each finger of the glove and you are set. It's a good idea to use thimbles of graduated sizes. Since thimbles offered for sale by magic shops are usually not sold by size, you can correct this by sticking in small strips of adhesive tape, pressing them firmly against the inside wall of the thimble, thus reducing the size of the thimble. Use one or more small strips of tape until the thimble feels just right for that particular finger. Then mark on the tape with a pen just which finger that thimble is for, and you need never think about it again.

Now for the routine in which the holder is used. You probably have your own ideas on this, but I prefer a short, snappy series of moves, on the theory that the only part of the trick that really means much is the production of the eight thimbles for the finale.

Beforehand, place a thimble on each finger of the right hand. Extend the forefinger and curl the other fingers into the palm, concealing the thimbles. No one will suspect their presence, because nobody knows what you plan to do. Just don't be self conscious about the extra thimbles.

Hold the right hand in front of the body, a little above the waist, with the thimble on the forefinger pointing to your left. Bring the left hand in front of the thimble and forefinger. The left hand is palm inward with the fingers pointing downward. Under cover of the left hand, thumb palm the thimble, straighten the

5.

forefinger again, close the left hand around it, and pretend to pull the thimble off. Turn slightly to the left, pretend to toss the thimble into the air and open the left hand. Pretend to catch the thimble by reproducing it on the right forefinger.

Hold the thimble and hands in position assumed at the start of the first vanish. With the same move pretend to remove the thimble and rub it against your coat at the right side of your chest. The right hand, meanwhile, holds the coat taut at the bottom of the right lapel. The fact that the right hand contains a thumb-palmed thimble and three others on the fingers need not interfere with this grip. Just keep the fingers curled and hold the edge of the coat with the thumb and bare forefinger.

Continue the rubbing motion against the coat with the left fist, then with an inward tossing motion open the left fingers wide and announce that the thimble has passed thru the cloth of your coat. Reach into the holder with the left hand and get the thimbles on the fingertips. As you bring the hand from beneath the coat, keep the forefinger extended to display the thimble, and the other fingers curled into the palm to conceal the other three.

Now execute the familiar effect of a thimble jumping from one forefinger to the other with the aid of the thumb palm. Then, after a pause, show all eight thimbles. You will find that this is a trouble-free way of performing a fine effect.

- - - - - -

COPPER AND SILVER

Here is a simplified version of an excellent effect in which a half dollar held by a spectator changes places with an English penny held by the performer. Previous methods depended either upon a faked coin or a switch which sometimes "talked". In this version the fake is dispensed with and the switch has been simplified so there is no possibility that the coins will clink together at an inopportune moment.

To begin, have an English penny in each of the side pockets of your coat. Stand behind a table, and place a chair to its right. Remove the coin from your left pocket and show it freely, calling attention to the fact that it has a heads and tails like American coins. This gives you a reason for showing both sides of the coin.

Remark that you also will need a half dollar; hold the penny in your left hand and dig into the right coat pocket as if in search of one. Palm the duplicate penny, remove the right

6.

hand from the pocket and take the visible penny between the right thumb and fingers, being careful not to expose the palm-ed coin.

With the left hand reach into your left coat pocket, as if still searching for a half dollar. Remark that you don't seem to have one, and ask for the loan of one. This procedure has en-abled you to palm a duplicate in a natural, unhurried manner.

When a spectator offers you a half dollar, seat him in the chair at your right. Place the half dollar and English penny on the table a few inches apart , the silver coin to your right. Ask the spectator to place his right hand palm upward on the table. Demonstrate with your left hand how he is to do this.

With your right hand pick up the half dollar, drop it on his palm and tell him to close his fist. Tell him that he closed it too slowly and ask him to open his hand again. Remove the coin from his palm into position for the regular palm. This can be accomplished easily by pressing the coin into the palm with the two left middle fingers as you turn the hand palm up. Dis-play the coin on your left hand and tell the spectator that you could have stolen the coin from him -- that he must close his hand more quickly.

While saying this, your right hand with the duplicate penny still palmed should rest on the table, or more specifically the tips of the right fingers and thumb should rest lightly on the table. Now you are set for the switch. Demonstrate how the spectator is to close his hand in this manner. Turn the left hand palm down and the right hand palm up beneath it, as if dumping the half dollar from your left palm into your right. (figure 3). But actually, you return the half dollar in your left palm.

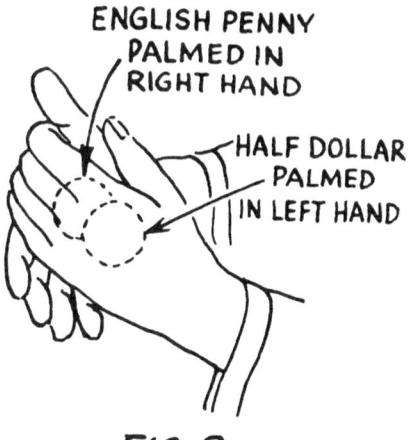

ENGLISH PENNY
PALMED IN
RIGHT HAND

HALF DOLLAR
PALMED
IN LEFT HAND

FIG. 3

Immediately close the right hand, move it slightly to the right and turn it palm down. Rest the tips of your left thumb and fingers on the ta-ble top. Properly timed, the illusion is perfect that you merely dumped the half dol-lar from your left hand to your right. Again turn the right hand palm up, but keep the fingers closed to conceal the coin. With the left fore-finger point to the closed

7.

right fingers and say: "In other words, close your hand quickly and turn it over so that I cannot get the coin away from you." As you say "turn it over" turn your right fist palm down again.

By this time the spectator should be thoroughly indoctrinated in the procedure. He also should be laboring under the delusion that your purpose is to try to snatch the coin away from him. Hence, he will never suspect that you are making a switch,and neither will anyone else if you have acted out this little drama properly.

To continue, place your right fist over his upturned right palm and drop the coin (presumably the half dollar but actually the duplicate penny) into his hand. Keep your right hand above his, concealing the coin, until he has closed his fingers and turned his fist palm down. You now have completed the crucial part of the trick.

With the right hand pick up the English penny from the table and get it into the right palm while displaying it in the same manner that you previously showed the half dollar in your left palm. Make the same " dumping " motion as before, only this time of course from the right hand to the left. With the closed left fist, touch the spectator's clenched fist and ask him if he felt anything. Tell him you made the coins change places. Have him open his hand and then open yours to reveal the transposition.

A simple dodge to get rid of the duplicate penny is to ask the spectator if the transposition is an "even trade". So saying, take the half dollar in your right and pretend to place it in your right coat pocket as if you intended to keep it. Instead, drop the palmed penny and withdraw the half, returning it to the spectator. This by-play usually gets a laugh.

This effect requires a certain amount of audacity, but like all tricks of this type, it makes a lasting impression on an audience. The effect usually is regarded as suitable only for close-up performances, but I have used it with good results before audiences of as many as 50 persons.

Even those who cannot clearly see the coins will be strongly impressed if you outline verbally each step of the procedure.

- - - - - - - - -

COINS AND GLASS

This is a pretty effect in which four coins pass into a glass. There have been several versions, but the one described here is perhaps the simplest and most direct.

As the audience sees it, four coins are counted and dumped into the right hand, the left hand seizing the glass. The right hand rubs the coins into the left elbow and one coin drops mysteriously into the glass. For the next coin, the procedure is reversed, the left hand rubbing a coin into the right elbow and a coin dropping into the glass. With two coins left, one is dropped openly into the glass and the other rubbed into the ear, only to land in the glass with its brothers.

The trick can be done with half dollars and an ordinary tumbler. However, for larger audiences, you may want to use silver dollars. In this case, use a thick-bottomed glass such as the bar glasses in which old fashions are mixed.

Set the glass on the table and hold the coins by their edges in a stack between the right fingers and thumb. Turn the right hand palm down. Place the bottom-most coin on the upturned left palm in position for palming and count, "one". Count the others into the left palm one at a time, dropping each with a clink so that it overlaps toward the left fingers.

Now, with the same tossing or dumping motion used in the preceding trick, dump the coins into the right hand, but retain the first coin counted in the left palm. The jingle of the other three falling into the right hand creates the illusion that all were thus transferred.

With the left hand, pick up the glass with the fingertips and thumb, the palm arching over the mouth of the glass (figure 4). Move the right fist to the inside crook of the left arm and pretend to rub the coins into the arm. Release the coin in the left hand so that it falls into the glass. Set the glass on the table. One coin has passed.

For the passage of the second coin, simply reverse the procedure, counting the coins into the right hand and dumping all but one into the left. Seize the glass with the right hand and rub the left fist against the right arm. Release the coin from the right palm and again set the glass on the table.

You now have two coins remaining in the left hand. Take one in the palm of each hand and display them for a moment. At

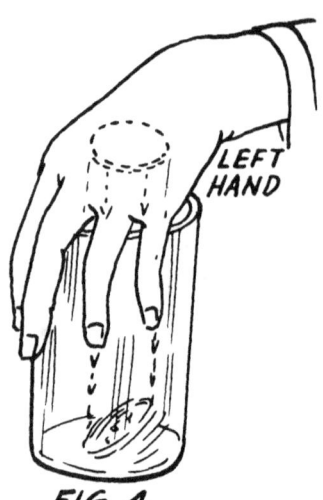

FIG. 4

this stage the glass should be direct
ly in front of you.

Tap the edge of the right hand coin
against the one in the left palm, then
drop it openly into the glass. Pretend to dump the left hand coin into
the right hand and immediately pick
up the glass with the left hand. Move
the closed right fist up to the right
ear and pretend to rub the coin into
the ear. Slap the ear with the right
palm and release the coin from the
left palm, letting it fall into the
glass to complete the effect.

- - - - - -

AN IMPROMPTU

Here is a closeup bit that is very easy to do on a moment's notice. In effect, three coins are shown and one is pocketed. The
other two are taken, one in each hand. The left hand coin is rubbed into the right elbow and joins the coin in the right hand. The
pocketed coin is then pulled invisibly thru the cloth of the trousers and mysteriously joins the other two.

To perform, place three half dollars in a row on the table. Announce that you will use only two to start with; pick up the one
on your right and pretend to place it in the right trouser pocket.
Actually palm it in the right hand, withdraw the hand from the
pocket and with the right second finger push the second coin a
few inches forward on the table. With the left hand push the
other coin forward, too.

Pick up the two tabled coins, one in each hand. Let the one in
the right hand rest on the curled fingers, the palmed coin above
it (figure 5). Press the one in the left hand into palming position and pretend to rub it into the inside crook of the right arm.
Release the coin in the right palm so that it falls upon the one
n the fingers with a clink.

Toss the two coins in the right hand onto the table and pick them
up with the left hand, which now has a coin palmed. Let the two
coins rest on the curved left fingers with the palmed coin above
them.

10.

RIGHT HAND

FIG. 5

Call attention to the fact (?) that one coin remains in the pocket. With the right thumb and forefingers pretend to pull it through the cloth of the trousers.

Hold up the imaginary coin for all to "see", and with a throwing motion pretend to toss it toward the left hand. Release the palmed coin with a clink and toss all three coins on the table.

- - - - - - - - -

A PENNY'S WORTH

In effect, a silver and copper coin are held in the left hand and the silver coin promptly passes into the right. It is rubbed into the left elbow and passes back into the left hand. Then it is placed in the left trouser pocket and pulled thru the cloth. Finally, the copper coin is squeezed and diminishes in size.

Have a U.S. penny in your left trouser pocket, a half dollar palmed in your left hand and another half dollar and an English penny on the table in front of you.

Place the half dollar and English penny on the right palm, the half dollar in palming position and the penny overlapping on top of it. Pretend to dump both coins into the left hand, retaining the half in the right palm and allowing only the penny to fall with a clink on the half in the left hand, which simultaneously turns palm up to catch it. This is a very illusory move. Apparently you have transferred both coins from the right hand to the left.

Show the two coins on the left palm. Close the left hand and turn it palm downwards, keeping the half in the palmed position. Close the right hand and hold it palm down a few inches from the left. The hands should be a couple of inches above the table top.

Order a coin to pass and let the half in the right hand drop on the table. Drop the English penny on the table, retaining the half palmed in the left hand. Rest the finger tips and thumbtips of both hands on the table as you pause to let the effect of the coin's apparent passage sink in.

11.

Pick up the half, pressing it into the right palm. Pick up the penny and hold it on the curled left fingers with the palmed half above it. Pretend to rub the half in the right hand into the left arm at the crook. Let the half in the left palm drop with a clink onto the penny, and drop the two coins in the left hand on the table. The half dollar apparently has passed back into the left hand.

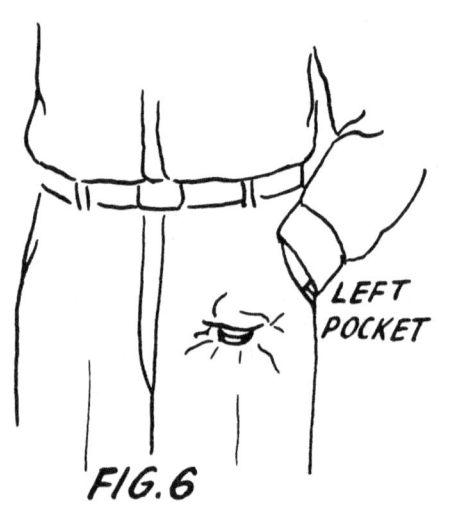

FIG.6

LEFT POCKET

For the next effect in the series, pick up the half dollar and place it in the left trouser pocket, taking this opportunity to get the U.S. penny in the finger palm position. With a coin of such small size, you can grip it at the root of the third finger alone. Leave the left hand in the pocket.

Pick up the English penny with the right hand and place its edge against the cloth of the trousers at the left pocket. Grasp the edge of the coin thru the cloth with the left thumb and forefinger, and remove the right hand for a moment. The coin is held in a crease in the cloth as in figure 6.

Grasp the coin again with the right hand, the two middle fingers below it and the thumb on top of it. Pull it sharply from the crease, letting go with the left hand, and let the half dollar in the right palm drop on the penny with a clink. The illusion is that you pulled the half dollar thru the cloth.

Drop both coins on the table and bring the left hand from the pocket, carrying with it the U.S. penny in the third finger grip. Pick up the English penny with the right hand, turning it palm up and pressing the coin into palming position. Pretend to dump the English penny into the left hand, retaining it in the right.

Pick up the half dollar with the right hand, announce that you are finished with it, and place it in the little change pocket in the right coat pocket. Let the palmed English penny fall into the larger section of the pocket.

Squeeze the penny in the closed left hand. Open the hand to
12.

show that the English penny has changed to a U.S. penny. Remark: "I must have squeezed too hard."

– – – – – – – – –

A QUICK OPENER

This is a routine I devised some time ago as a novel way of
opening a program of small effects. The idea was derived from
the customary type of opening used by many big illusionists,
who launch at once into a fast series of colorful effects.

Applying the same principle on a smaller scale, the sleight of
hand performer enters, looks at his watch and announces he
will attempt three tricks in exactly thirty seconds. He whips a
red silk from a tumbler on his table, shakes it and a knot appears. He takes a golf ball from a tumbler, swallows it and
reproduces it from beneath his coat. Lastly, he takes two silver dollars from the tumbler, drops one of them back, twists
the other into his ear and it appears in the glass with a re-
sounding clink.

That is the effect. Actually, any three quickies could be used,
but those outlined above have proved quite effective. The routine also can be used as an interlude instead of an opener. For
instance, it can be used effectively after a series of opening
card effects to change the pace and get into the performance
of tricks with other objects.

Most readers probably are familiar with the moves in this
series of three quick effects. The best way to knot the silk is
Dr. Tarbell's simplified method. The silk is twisted rope fashion and laid across the right palm. The left hand seized the
corner that dangles behind the right hand.

The left hand brings this corner up quickly in front of the right
hand, and the corner is clipped between the right first and
second fingers. The right hand then shakes the silk downward
and the knot is tied automatically. In performance, all the moves
are blended into a single shake.

You can use any sleight you like to simulate the swallowing of
the ball. I like to display it on the top of the right fist. Bring
the fist up to the mouth and pretend to swallow the ball. When
the mouth covers the ball, let it roll down into the fist and
palm it. Stick out your tongue to simulate the ball's presence
inside the mouth. Pretend to swallow it and reproduce it from
beneath your vest. The final effect with the two silver dollars
will be recognized as the finale of the trick with the four coins
and the glass described earlier. It is the most deceptive of

13.

the three effects and should be used last.

- - - - - - -

A KNIFE MOVE

If you use the color changing knives, you will like this little sucker effect. It can be used as a finale for some short routines or it can be employed to build up a longer routine.

Effect: After several color changes in the usual manner, the knife is laid flat on the fingers of the left hand and the spectators are asked to watch it more closely. The right hand is seen to make a suspicious move as if stealing the knife away or substituting another.

The hand then travels beneath the left arm and presumably deposits the knife there. The left hand is closed as if containing a substitute knife. The left hand is then opened to show that the knife has changed color. Finally, the left arm is raised away from the side of the body and the knife presumably placed there has gone.

Method: Actually, of course, there is only one knife, of the color changing variety. After performing several changes and showing both sides of the knife with the familiar "paddle" move, lay the knife across the left fingers. Place the right hand directly over the knife, lengthwise, as if palming it. Move the right hand away and close the left hand, causing the knife to turn over so that when the hand is opened it can be shown to have changed color.

The right hand, held suspiciously as if it were palming a knife, moves to place it beneath the left armpit. The hand is then removed and the left arm is held tightly against the side of the body. Open the left hand and show that the knife has changed color. Then, lift the left arm.

This is nothing more than a simple ruse, but properly performed it can be highly effective.

- - - - - - - -

BOB LOTZ' COLOR CHANGING KNIVES

Magicians who have seen Bob Lotz' masterful knife routine are unanimous in their praise. It is a bewildering series of effects with a fine surprise to conclude the sequence. Bob has been kind enough to let me have the moves for this book, thus making this excellent routine available to you.

14.

Place a small white knife, little more than an inch long, in the left coat pocket. In the right coat pocket, place a black, stag handled knife, a white handled knife and the fake knife, black on one side, white on the other. Because of the rough texture of the stag handle, the three knives can easily be distinguished by touch.

I shall let Bob Lotz describe the working, as follows:

Take black knife out of right coat pocket and let it roll over several times in right hand as you explain that you "like to do this trick because all you need is a pocket knife (replace black in right coat pocket) which you can easily carry in your pocket. Then, whenever anyone asks you to do a trick (again place right hand into right coat pocket, but this time remove fake knife, black side up) all you have to do is reach into your pocket and pull out the knife."

Hold fake between thumb and first finger of right hand ready to do the turnover move. Rub fake on left coat sleeve "to generate static electricity". Do turnover as you place fake still black side up across left palm. Shut left hand, turn it palm down, move it a little to the right and back again (reason given later), push fake out with left thumb and remove with right hand showing that fake has now changed to white. Repeat those moves changing fake to black again.

Explain that "as you probably guessed, two knives are used. One is in the hand and the other is here in the pocket". As you say this, place right hand containing fake into right coat pocket, drop fake and come out with black and white. Take white in left and black in right hand and slowly show both sides of both knives.

Replace black in right coat pocket, start color changing routine, then remember that "we started with the black knife in the left hand, didn't we?" With right hand, remove fake from right coat pocket, black side up, place in left hand with blades toward fingertips, remove white from left hand and place in right coat pocket.

Start color changing routine calling attention to the fact that "rubbing the knife on the coat sleeve has nothing to do with the trick. Notice this little movement of the left hand? That exchanges the knives so that we now have the white knife in the left hand (show fake white side up) and the black knife here in the pocket. " Reach into right coat pocket with right hand and remove black, showing both sides casually. Replace black in right coat pocket and repeat this entire procedure, this time ending up with fake black side up in left hand and removing white from right coat pocket.

White is now placed in left hand in front of fake, both knives with blades toward left fingertips as you state that "some people don't seem to understand how the knives change places - so I'll explain. All you have to remember is that the black knife is always kept in the left hand."

Point to fake with right forefinger, close left hand and turn it palm down. With right hand, pull fake (now white side up) part way out of left hand, being careful not to allow white to be seen. Turn right hand palm up. Clip fake between right thumb and middle of right forefinger and pull fake into right hand, allowing it to lie across the fingers. Remark that "the white knife is in the right hand."

As you say this, shut the fingers of the right hand, thus turning fake so that black side is up. "And the black knife is in the left hand." As you say this, turn the left hand over, palm up, but still shut. Move the hands slightly toward each other and back again "in order to switch the knives ". Open the right hand showing that it now contains the black knife (fake) and as you open left hand to show white, casually allow the knife to roll over several times.

"Of course, I just used two knives for demonstrating purposes. When doing the trick, only one knife should be shown." Place fake black side up across left palm with blades toward finger-tips and white in front of fake in the same manner. Shut left hand, turn it palm down and remove fake (now white side up) with right hand, saying "black knife in left hand and white knife in the pocket." Place fake in right coat pocket.

" Of course nobody knows that two knives are used." Make a lateral movement with left hand, open left hand and allow white to roll over several times. With right hand, reach into coat pocket (right one), remove black and show that knives have again changed places.

Hold each knife between thumb and first finger of each hand with other fingers loosely closed. State that "some performers prefer to keep one knife in each coat pocket so that they won't get scratched." While saying this, place right hand with black into right coat pocket and left hand with white into left coat pocket. Close last three fingers of left hand around the small knife. Immediately bring both hands out of pockets.

16.

"Whether you keep the knives in separate pockets or not, never show both knives at the same time. If you do, I'll show you what will happen." Place black into right coat pocket. Take white in right hand and allow left hand to hang loosely in front of chest with small knife lying across loosely curled fingers.

"Suppose we wanted to change the color of the white knife." Shut left hand tightly with back up, knuckles to the front. With palm of right hand toward body, grasp white (blades up) between thumb and middle finger and allow tips of first and third fingers to go on top and bottom of knife. Keep right fingers close together.

Place outside tip of white against right side of curled up left forefinger as tho to insert white into left hand. Quickly push right fingers along knife until they hit left hand. (If done rapidly, this gives a perfect illusion of pushing white into left fist.) Immediately straighten right hand, keeping white tightly gripped between first and third fingers, thumb relaxed.

Keeping back of right hand to audience, reach into right coat pocket, drop white and bring out black. "If you should happen to show the black knife while the white knife is in the left hand (replace black in right coat pocket and come out with empty right hand) the white knife won't change color, it will change size."

Hold left hand palm up, open it and allow small knife to fall on cocktail table. Sip your martini while spectators regain their senses!

If carefully done, this routine may be performed surrounded by the audience. The only thing that will lick you is a drunk lying on the floor looking up!

Does this seem like a complicated routine? Well, it is. And it may take quite a while before you can do it without straining your memory. But it's worth it!

- - - - - -

DOUBLE COUNT

Effect: Spectator and performer both select cards. Deck is dealt into two piles. Each selected card is found at the same number from the top of each pile.

Method: Note the bottom card as your key card and spread the deck for a spectator to select a card. When he does, close the spread, undercut half the deck and let him replace his card on what originally was the top half. Drop the other half on top.

The deck now can be given a short overhand shuffle provided you are careful not to separate the key from the selected card. Next turn the deck faces toward yourself and spread the cards. Cut to bring the key to the top.

Turn the deck face down, show the key card and announce that it is the card you will select. Replace it on top and cut the deck to bring it to the middle. Deal the entire deck, a card at a time, into two piles, the first card to your left, the second to the right and so forth.

Pick up the right hand half, spread it with the faces toward the spectator and ask him if he sees his card. If he does, hand him the packet and pick up the other half. Each of you holds his packet face down.

Instruct him to deal the cards face down in unison as you deal yours. But you must turn each card you deal face up. When you have dealt your selected card, call attention to it and halt the deal. Have him name his card and turn up the last one he dealt. It is his selected card.

If the spectator's card is not in the right hand half when you show it to him after dealing to divide the pack, simply close the spread, slip one card from the top to the bottom and hand him the other half. Proceed with the unison deal as before.

- - - - - -

FLIP OVER

Effect: A selected card is discovered in rapid fire manner with the aid of the Ace of Spades.

Method: Secretly get the Ace of Spades to the top. Have a selection made, undercut half the pack and let the spectator drop his card on top of the ace. Drop the other half on top.

Cut the deck a couple of times, then announce you will need the Ace of Spades. Spread the deck faces toward you, find the ace and cut to bring it to the top. This brings the selected card to the bottom, or face of the deck.

Turn the deck face down, being careful not to expose the selected card and turn the Ace of Spades face up on top. Hand it to the spectator and ask him to insert it anywhere he likes, face up, as you cut the cards. Execute the Hindu shuffle with the pack face down and when he drops the ace face up on the left hand portion, drop the remainder of the cards in the right hand on top.

Spread the deck face down and remark that the spectator had a perfectly free choice in replacing the ace anywhere he chose. Cut to bring the face up ace to the top again. Hold the deck in the left hand with the thumb on top and the fingers below, the fingertips on the face of the bottom card.

Toss the deck sharply into the right hand. The top and bottom cards will remain in the left hand. Have the spectator name his card, turn the two cards over and drop them on the table, displaying the selected card behind the ace.

- - - - - - -

UPSIDE DOWN SHUFFLE

Here is a novel effect based on a more elaborate version shown to me a few years ago by Ed Marlo and Martin Gardner.

In effect, the spectator chooses a card by calling "stop" as the magician riffles the deck. The pack is then divided and half turned face up. The two halves are riffle shuffled and the face down half is pulled clear thru the other. But one face down card is seen to have remained in the face up half. It is the selected card.

To perform, hold the deck in position for the spectator peek as known to most card addicts, in which the spectator peeks at the index corner of a card and performer secures a break with the flesh of the little finger. The deck is held in dealing position but slightly beveled to the right, with the left thumb pressing on the back.

Place the tip of the right second finger against the right edge of the deck, near the outer corner, and riffle by bending the cards upward and letting them escape from the fingertip. Halt the riffle when the spectator calls stop. If you time the riffle properly, this should be somewhere near the middle.

Hold a temporary break at this point with the right second fingertip so that the spectator can note the card. Then, continue the riffle, letting the rest of the cards escape the fingertip, but hold a break beneath the selected card with the fleshy part of the left little fingertip. There is no need to insert the little fingertip into the break. Just press it tightly against the lower half.

Pause a moment after selection of the card, then spread the cards above the break between the hands, commenting that the spectator could have chosen any card in the pack.

Maintain the little finger break and turn over all cards above the selected one so that they are face up on top of the lower half. Move all cards above the break, including the face down selected card, about an inch to the right, and hold the two packets in this stepped position by pressure of the left thumb, figure 8. Remark that half the cards face one way and half the other.

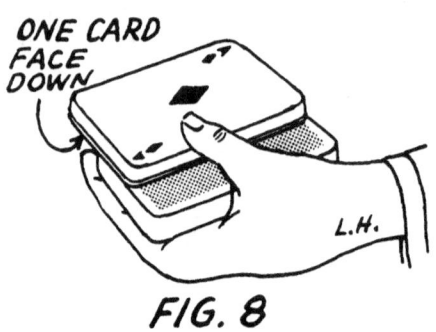

ONE CARD
FACE
DOWN

L.H.

FIG. 8

Actually, the selected card, face down, is the bottom card of the face up half.

With the right hand, cut off half of the face up cards and place them on the table. Place the rest of the face up cards on top of them. This brings the face down selected card to the middle of the face up half, unknown to the audience. Cut the face down half in similar fashion, placing it to the left of the face up half.

Now riffle shuffle the two packets together at an angle. The best way to do this is to hold the cards by the sides, riffling the long edges with the thumbs as professional dealers do.

Push the face down half thru the face up half, diagonally, pull it clear thru the face up half and set it aside. The cards should be shuffled into each other almost at right angles. Don't try to make it look like a good strip-out false shuffle.

Now spread the face up half ribbon-wise on the table, disclosing one card face down. Tell the spectators it "got stuck" there during the shuffle. Ask the name of the selected card and exe-

cute the familiar ribbon turnover to show that the reversed
card is the selected one.

- - - - - - - -

A   TRANSPOSITION

Magicians and laymen alike seem to enjoy effects in which objects change places, especially if it is quite apparent that no
duplicates are used. Here is a direct method of performing the
effect in which two cards change places.

Get a seven, for instance, the seven of Spades, on top of the
deck. Place the eight of the same suit above it. Double lift to
show the seven, turn the two cards as one face down and place
the eight in the right trouser pocket, holding it by the index corner. When the card is halfway into the pocket turn it face out-
ward. Actually it is the eight but will be taken for the seven.

Double lift again, showing an indifferent card, for instance the
ace of hearts. Leave the two cards as one face up on top. Turn
the left hand palm down, bringing the deck in position for the
glide. Execute the glide, withdrawing the second card in the
usual manner. The fact that this card is face down and the deck
face up makes the sleight even more convincing.

Push this card, presumably the ace of hearts but actually the
seven of spades, into the center of the deck. The deck is face
up and the card goes in face down. Leave it protruding a frac-
tion of an inch and turn the left hand slightly with its palm toward your body.

With the straightened right fingers, push the card flush,figure
9. Turn the left hand palm up and palm the ace of hearts in
your right hand. You can use any palming method you like.

Raise the deck to shoulder
height and riffle its edge sharply with your left thumb.Plunge
the right hand into the pocket
and draw forth the palmed
ace of hearts, which you apparently just pushed into the
deck. Spread the deck and
show the seven of spades face
up in the center.

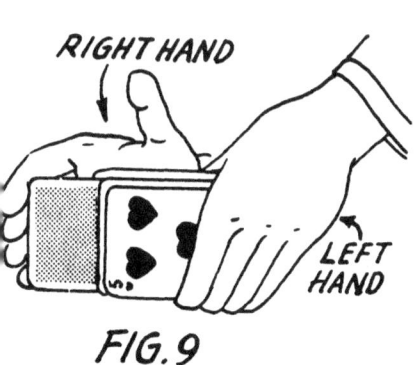

RIGHT HAND

LEFT
HAND

FIG. 9

- - - - - -

21.

Another way of accomplishing the foregoing effect is to use the side steal. Begin as before, double lifting to show the seven of spades and placing the eight in the pocket. Double lift again to show the ace of hearts and leave the two cards as one face up on top.

Grip the deck from above with the right hand, fingers at the outer end and thumb at the inner end. As you take this grip, pull up with the ball of the right thumb on the inner edge of the upturned ace of hearts, separating it from the rest of the deck, and hold this break with the flesh of the thumb.

The deck is still held by the left hand, too. Carry away the bottom half of the pack in the left hand, moving it to the left, and slide this portion up and over the half held from above by the right hand. Figure 10 shows this action nearly completed.

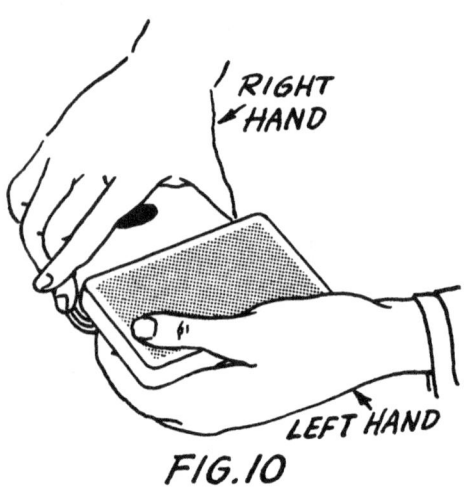

RIGHT HAND

LEFT HAND

FIG. 10

Readers may recognize this move as the first part of the sleight known as the double cut. The right thumb still holds the break beneath the ace of hearts, and when the deck is reassembled after the cut, the left little finger takes up the break.

As the spectators see it, you merely have cut the ace of hearts to the middle, but the deck is now in position for the side steal.

No detailed explanation of the side steal need be given here. Suffice it to say that the card is pushed into the palm of the right hand by straightening the left little finger. This pushes the card diagonally from the deck, starting it on its way.

The two middle fingers of the left hand give it another push in to the right palm. The entire operation is covered by the right hand, which maintains its grip on opposite ends of the deck throughout the sleight. Once the card is palmed, raise the deck in the left hand, riffle as before and terminate the trick as in the preceding version.

- - - - - - - -

A SANDWICH

In " For Card Men Or˙y", I gave a couple of methods of perfor·
ming the so-called " sandwich" effect. Spectators seem to like
this general effect, and further experimentation has produced
the following version, somewhat different in pattern.

Openly remove the red deuces, call attention to them and place
them on the table, having two spectators each select a card.
With the pack in the left hand, hold the red deuces face up in
the right hand and have the first spectator place his card between them, face down.

Square the three cards by sliding them onto the top of the deck,
and get a break beneath the top face up deuce. Now execute
the sleight known as the double cut. For those who are not
familiar with it, here is the only explanation needed: grip the
deck from above with the right hand, fingers at the outer end
and thumb at the inner end. The right thumb takes and holds
the break beneath the top deuce. The left hand maintains its
grip on the deck in the dealing position.

Announce that you will cut the cards a couple of times to mix
them up. Carry the bottom half of the deck away to the left in
the left hand as in the earlier trick entitled " Another Method"
and complete the cut as in figure 10. Now, simply cut at the
break and the sleight is completed. This brings the face up
red deuce to the bottom, the selected card face down on top,
and the other deuce face up beneath it.

Now, have the second spectator place his card on top. He will
never realize he is placing it atop the first spectator's card.
Get a break beneath the two selected cards and execute only
the first half of the double cut, bringing the two selected cards
to the center with a break beneath them.

Ask the first spectator if he is concentrating on his card and
execute the side steal as explained in " Another Method". For
further explanations of this valuable sleight, see " Art of Magic
and " Expert Card Technique".

With the first spectator's card in the right palm upon comple -
tion of the side steal, turn slightly to the left, raise the deck
in the left hand, riffle and produce the palmed card from the
right trouser pocket. This is the card that originally formed
the center of the " sandwich".

Run thru the deck face down and show that there is still one card between the face up deuces in the center. Withdraw these three cards, ask spectator No. 2 to name his card, and show that it is sandwiched between the deuces.

- - - - - - - - - -

COUNT DOWN

Here is a simple, non-sleight effect which always creates amusement. In effect, the performer attempts to locate a selected card by executing a running cut, letting the spectator call "stop" whenever he likes. But the card stopped at is a seven. Counting down seven cards, the magician finds the selected card.

Beforehand, get any seven-spot seven cards from the bottom. The seven is a good card to use, but you can use any other spot card providing it is not so small that it kills the counting effect.

Spread the deck for a selection. Close the spread and undercut half the deck, letting the spectator replace his card on what was the top half. Drop the other half on top.

Square the cards meticulously, pause and ask the spectator if he is sure his card is still in the deck. "Let's make absolutely sure", you say, and spread the cards slowly, face up, so that he can see his card. Spread until you come to the seven.

In closing the spread, get a little finger break beneath this card and cut at the break to bring the seven to the top, or rear, of the deck. Now execute a Hindu shuffle with the deck face up and tell the spectator to stop whenever he likes. When he calls "stop", carefully place the portion remaining in the right hand on the packet in the left, but injog the top packet about half its length.

Do this in a manner to demonstrate clearly that you are employing no sleight of hand. In the same manner, turn the entire deck face down. The injogged packet now will be beneath the other. As if you were handling soap bubbles, place the injogged packet on top.

This is a wierd move, but for some reason people think you have cut to the top the card at which you were stopped. Actually you have cut the seven to the top. Turn it face up, as if fully expecting to have it be acknowledged as the selected card.

Then, after feigning embarrassment, count down to the seventh card and disclose it as the long sought card the spectator chose.

24.

ACE LOCATION

Effect: Four aces are lost in the deck. One is found by spelling, two by cutting. The performer tries to find the last ace by having a spectator call "stop" during a running cut, and turns up a seven. He counts down seven cards and finds the missing ace.

Method: Actually this is an elaboration of the preceding effect. Run thru the deck and cut to bring a seven to the face. Continue spreading and remove the four aces, assembling them at the face of the deck.

Reading from left to right, they should be assembled in this order: The two red aces, the ace of clubs and the ace of spades. The order of the red aces is immaterial.

The above arrangement is made openly. After the cards have been set up, spread the deck again to show the aces. Don't comment about the seven, but continue spreading, ostensibly to show that the deck is shuffled.

Starting with the seven, count seven cards as you spread and get a left little finger break beneath the seventh card counted. Close the deck, maintaining the break. With the deck face up, execute the double cut as explained earlier. Follow this with a false shuffle or cut, and show that no ace is at the top or bottom of the pack.

Announce that you will find the ace of clubs by spelling its name. Spell a-c-e-o-f-c-l-u-b-s, dealing a card for each letter, and turn up the card at "s" to reveal the ace of clubs. This works out automatically because of the set up. Replace the dealt cards, whose order will now be reversed, on top of the deck. Unknown to the audience, this brings the two red aces to the top.

Get a break under the top ace and again execute the double cut. Show a red ace on top and turn the pack face up to show the other red ace on the bottom. With the deck face up, execute a Hindu shuffle and ask a spectator to call "stop". Finish the trick with the sucker finish exactly as described in the preceding effect.

You will find that this is one of the easiest of all four ace effects, yet a very effective one.

- - - - - - -

AN AMBITIOUS CARD

This sequence of ambitious card moves was designed with the idea of holding the use of the double lift to a minimum. The double lift is a valuable sleight, but it should not be overdone. In this arrangement, a card appears at the top of the deck four times, yet the double lift is used only twice.

Method: Ask a spectator his favorite card. Suppose he says the Ace of Spades. Run thru the deck and cut the ace to the face. Get a left little finger break beneath the second card from the face. Announce that you will cut a couple of times to bury the ace and execute the double cut, with the deck face up. Turn the deck face down and show that the ace is not on top.

Command the ace to rise to the top, double lift, and show that it has arrived. Turn the two cards as one face down, remove the top card and without showing its face, push it into the middle of the deck.

Again order the ace to rise, turn over the top card and show it to be the ace. This time, announce that you will place it second from the top. Do so, and get a break beneath the two top cards.

Again order the ace to the top, turn up the two top cards as one and disclose the ace, apparently on top. Turn the two cards as one face down, remove the top card and push it into the center. Order it to rise again, turn up the top card and show that the ace has carried out your command.

From this point, you can proceed with other methods requiring sleights other than the double lift. Or you can conclude the routine at this point. People who haven't seen a lot of card tricks regard this short demonstration as quite remarkable.

- - - - -

ACE - KING A LA MARLO

Here is Ed Marlo's improved handling of an effect from my book " For Card Men Only, " explained here with his kind permission.

Effect, four aces are dealt on the table, one face up, the others face down. A king is dealt beside them. The face up ace is removed and placed in the center of the deck. The other aces mysteriously follow it. The three face down cards beside the king are found to have changed to kings.

26.

Method: Secretly get the four kings to the top. You can do this while running thru the deck to remove the aces. Hold the deck face down in the left hand and get a little finger break beneath the four kings. With the right hand place the aces face up on top of the deck as if to square them. Grasp all eight cards above the break with the right hand, fingers at the outer end and thumb at the inner end.

The fingers should completely screen the outer edge of the cards. Next , move these eight cards (presumably only the four aces) to the right, so that the left edge of this small packet rests near the right edge of the deck, overlapping.

Place the left thumb tip on the face of the top ace near its left edge. Move the rest of the small packet slightly more to the right, then use it to flip the first ace over so that it lands face down on top of the deck, figure 11. As you flip the ace over, call its suit. Repeat the move, calling each ace by its suit until you have one ace left in the right hand with the kings concealed beneath it. Place it and the hidden kings beneath it squarely on top of the deck, the ace still face up.

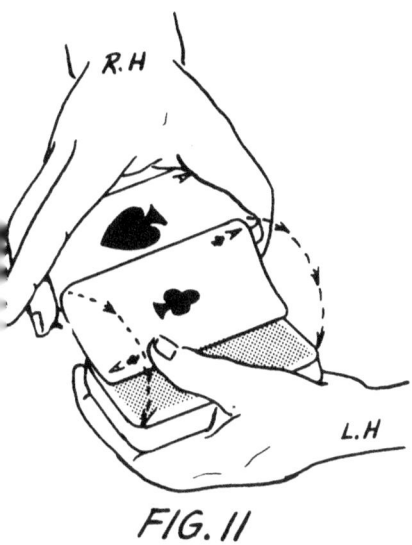

R.H

L.H

FIG. II

The audience will believe that the four aces are on top,with the top aces face up. Actually the four kings are beneath the top ace.

Deal this ace face up on the table, and deal three kings (ostensibly aces) face down on top of it, each card overlapping in a spread. Turn the next card face up and remark that t happens to be a king. Showing this card tends to convince your audience that the cards on the table are all aces.

Deal this king face up, overlapping on the cards on the table. Ask a spectator to cut the deck into two heaps. Slide the face up ace from beneath the other tabled cards and place it face up on what was the top half. Thus it goes on top of the other three aces, unknown to the audience. Complete the cut, burying the ace in the middle.

Riffle the deck and spread to the face up ace. Deal it on the table and deal the next three cards, the aces, face up on top of it. With the face up king, flip over the three face down cards to show that they have changed to kings.

In the original version of this effect, it was necessary to have three kings secretly turned face up at the start. But this handling by Ed Marlo, characterized by the smoothness and subtlety that has become his trademark, has placed the trick in the impromptu class, the most desirable category of all card effects. - - - - - - -

AN UNSCRUPULOUS DEAL

Effect: Magician seeks to find selected card by dealing face up, but he stops at the wrong card. Unperturbed, he deals the selected card, apparently from nowhere.

Method: This is the best use I have ever found for the second deal, at least from the point of view of entertainment.

Note the top card as your key, spread the deck for a selection and undercut three-fourths of the deck or more. Let the spectator drop his card on top of what was the top portion, and complete the cut. This brings his card above your key.

False shuffle if you like, then turn the deck face up and begin dealing, asking the spectator to watch for his card. When the key appears as the face card of those in the left hand, halt the deal and ask the spectator if this is his card. When he replies that it is not, have him name his card and produce it by means of the second deal. The effect may never become a classic, but it invariably produces a laugh.
- - - - - - - -

SPOT REMOVER

Effect: A card is rubbed face to face with the three of clubs and the three becomes a deuce. The other card is shown to be the ace of clubs, representing the missing spot. After a little more by-play, the deuce changes back to the three. This really is a very bewildering switch, for which I claim no originality except for its adaptation.

A slight setup is involved, but trick makes an excellent opener and the scant trouble in setting up the cards is well worth while.

Place the three face down on top, the deuce face up on top of it and the ace face down on top of all. Put the pack in its case and you are set.

To present, remove the pack from its case and get a break beneath the two top cards. Grasp these two cards as one with the right hand, second finger at the outer edge, thumb at the inner edge, and the first finger curled against the back of the top card.

Remove the two cards as one, carrying them slightly to the right. Push off the trey with the left thumb, and using the double card as a lever flip it face up on top of the deck. Call its name and with the left thumb push it off the pack and beneath the double card in the right hand, so that it "underlaps" as in figure 12.

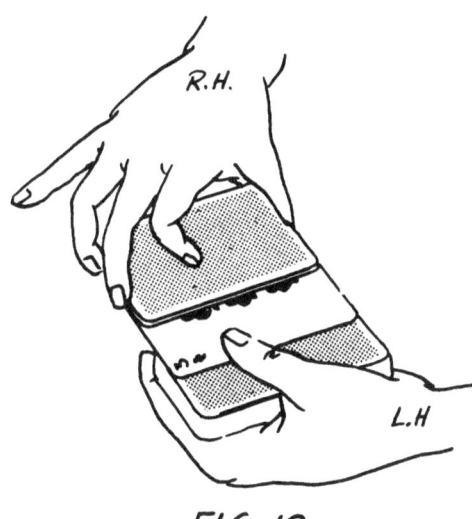

R.H.

L.H

FIG. 12

Next, square the three cards, (ostensibly two) on the top of the deck, getting a left little finger break beneath them. With the tip of the right second finger, slide the top face down card toward yourself, revealing the deuce as in figure 13.

Then place the injogged card face up on the table, showing it to be the ace. Patter to the effect that the ace is the spot you rubbed off.

You still have a little finger break beneath the two

face up cards on top of the deck, so turn them face down as if they were a single card. Deal the top card, presumably the deuce, but actually the trey, face down on the table.

Pick up the ace and place it face down on top of the deck. Demonstrate how you can transfer the spot back again by pressing

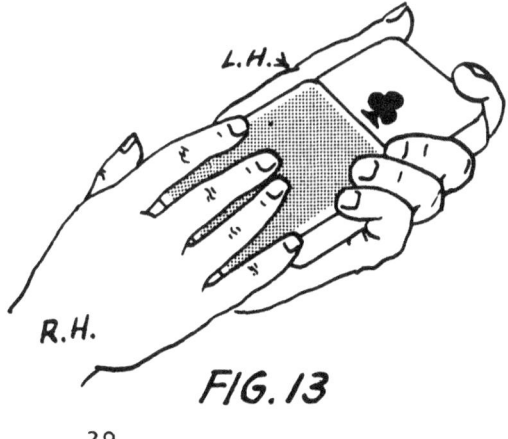

L.H.

R.H.

FIG. 13

your right thumbtip first against the back of the ace at its
center, and then against the back of the tabled card, precisely
at its center.

Turn the tabled card face up to disclose that it has changed
back to the trey.

. . . .

Introduction

By

TOM OSBORNE

In the quiet sanctum of one's home, or in a circle of intimate friends, a person performing an effect in magic may be perfectly at ease, but under fire before a critical audience it may be a different story. More times than I care to remember I have seen this happen; this is especially true of the spare-time Magician and, believe me, it is my sincere desire to help overcome this failing.

I do not believe a person can be made into a successful Magician, and when I speak of a successful Magician, I mean one who lives on magic and magic alone, year in and year out, and always in constant demand for his services. I firmly believe a successful Magician is born, not made.

But, I also believe a person can be taught to perform Magician's tricks in a manner that is quite pleasing. It is with this thought in mind that I have consented to put into print my version of the routines that are in this book; some are old, and some are of my origination, to the old tricks, we hope we have added something that will give you added pleasure for the rest of your lives.

Published By

D. ROBBINS & COMPANY, INC.

127 WEST 17TH STREET

NEW YORK, N. Y. 10011

CLINK　　　　　　　**STUCK**

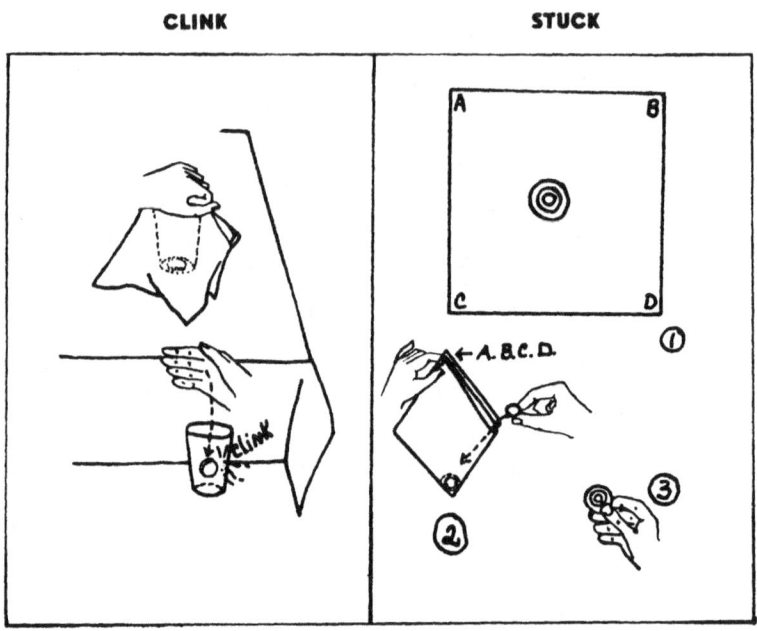

CLINK

REMARKS: This is a very mysterious trick, and just because the description may seem absurd do not be deceived into thinking it ridiculous.

EFFECT: The performer, after covering a glass with a napkin, calls attention to a half dollar which he holds in his right hand; he now claims he can pass the coin into the glass without touching the glass or the napkin. After tapping the coin on the table to prove its solidarity, it is transferred to the left hand, which then makes a throwing motion toward the glass and the coin is heard to arrive. When the napkin is removed, the coin is seen resting in the bottom of the glass.

STUCK

REMARKS: This is essentially an after dinner trick, and unless it is performed with exactness, it is scarcely worth showing. It demands of the tricktrician a certain amount of boldness for perfect presentation.

EFFECT: The performer first collects ten pennies from the spectators; these are placed into his right side coat pocket; next he borrows a dime, a quarter, and a nickel. These latter three are placed into a pile in the center of a napkin. The performer now gathers up the four corners to form a bag and drops into it the ten pennies, and if you are following closely this will total fifty cents. He now removes the quarter from the bag; it disappears and yet when the bag is opened fifty cents are found inside.

CLINK

HERE'S HOW: Secretly hide a glass in your lap with the mouth upwards; now await an opportunity when no one is looking and sneak a half dollar into an empty glass, which is on the table and immediately cover it with a napkin. As soon as this is accomplished, call attention to a duplicate coin in your right hand; now make your favorite "PASS", retaining the coin in the right hand; the left hand, which apparently holds the coin, is held about a foot over the covered glass, while the right hand, which is hiding the palmed coin, moves backwards until it is directly over the glass which is in your lap.

Make a throwing motion with your left hand toward the covered glass, and at the termination of the movement, open the left hand, and simultaneously drop the coin into the glass which is in your lap. This creates a perfect illusion of the coin going through the napkin; remove the napkin and show the coin in the bottom.

STUCK

HERE'S HOW: Roll forty pennies in tissue paper and place them in your right side pocket; now stick some wax or chewing gum on both sides of a nickel; this is placed into the vest pocket.

Spread a napkin out on the table, and ask the spectators to contribute by tossing ten pennies onto the napkin; now gather up the ten pennies and place them in the pocket which contains the roll of forty. Bring out the sticky nickel and ask someone to lay a quarter in the center of the napkin; lay your nickel on top of it and request someone to place a dime on top of the nickel; see No. 1.

The performer gathers up the napkin to form a bag, as in No. 2; the right goes into the pocket and brings out the ten pennies and the roll which he keeps hidden in the loosely held fist; now drop the ten pennies into the bag one at a time so you will have a total of fifty cents; starting at forty, count each aloud, and as soon as you say "fifty" plunge your hand into the bag, leaving the roll of pennies inside and bring out the three coins that are stuck together, holding them up as if they were but the quarter, as in No. 3.

Ask someone to hold the bag by the corners, and you make a "PASS" with the supposed quarter towards the bag. With your free hand you feel through the cloth, as if to ascertain if the coin has arrived; this is done for the purpose of unloosening the paper around the forty coins, and as soon as this is done, you offer to bet anyone that there are fifty cents in the bag. Invite someone to feel through the cloth; if the napkin is heavy enough, he will not notice the extra pennies and the tissue paper will pass unnoticed. They are feeling for the quarter, and when they are satisfied it is not in the bag you conclude by taking away the napkin from the spectator, with one hand holding the corners while the other hand holds the napkin by the bottom so as to grasp the paper through the cloth; now shake the fifty pennies on the table and collect your bet.

HAND TO HAND   COIN PRODUCTION

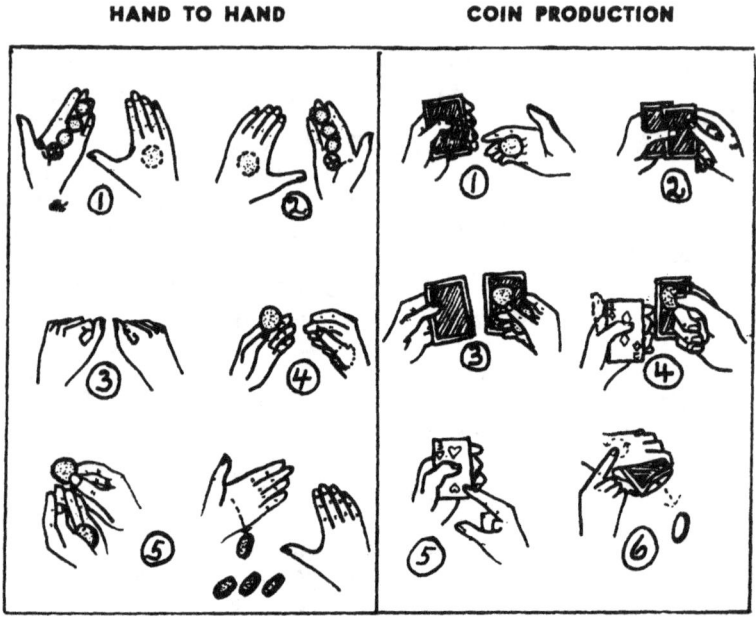

HAND TO HAND

REMARKS: This is a very brilliant sleight-of-hand trick when perfectly performed. It requires of the performer a combination of skill and continuity, and by practicing the routine as a whole you can obtain both.

EFFECT: Four large size coins are made to pass one at a time from one fist to another without any one knowing how it was done.

COIN PRODUCTION

REMARKS: On the first attempt you may be inclined to say this is impossible to do, but I assure you that after you get the knack of it you will find it as easy as one, two, three. The thrill you receive when you see the look of astonishment on the faces of the spectators when they see the coins appearing will more than recompense you for the effort involved.

EFFECT: The performer shows two playing size cards on both sides; the two cards are placed together; presently a large size coin is seen to drop from the cards', this is repeated several times.

HAND TO HAND

HERE'S HOW: Begin by showing four coins in the left hand, the right hand hides an extra one. You now say, "I shall invisibly pass the coins, one at a time, from one hand to the other."

No. 2: Throw the left hand coins over to the right with the exception of the X coin which is· retained and hidden by palming; close both hands into fists, and after a moment, open the left hand, letting its coin drop on the table. Now count three coins into the left palm, adding the extra coin at the word three and immediately close the left hand into a fist to hide it; this maneuver permits the right hand to be shown empty; now count back from the left fist three coins, retaining one as before; again both hands go into fists; once more the left hand opens and drops a coin. The right hand now counts over but two coins into the left palm, then, as at first, the left hand throws over (apparently) its coins, but retains one by palming, the coin striking against the one in the right hand produces the effect that two coins were thrown over. Once more the hands go into a fist, and again the left hand drops a coin on the table.

The right hand throws over one coin, being careful not to betray the fact that you have two coins; now a move known to magicians as the change over palm is executed, the left hand holds its coin as in No. 4; the extra one is hidden in the right hand by palming.

Openly remove the left coin as illustrated in No. 5, secretly dropping the hidden right one, the left hand going into a fist as soon as it receives it; now make the right hand into a fist and finish by dropping the left hand coin, and get rid of the extra coin when picking up the coins from the table.

COIN PRODUCTION

HERE'S HOW: The left hand holds two cards, while the right hand palms four coins; see No. 1. Push over one card, as in No. 2; notice the position of the right fingers; the right thumb now pushes up one coin to the back of the card, as in No. 3. Turn the left hand card face up, the left thumb moving backward so the right hand can lay its card and the hidden coin down on the left card, as in Nos. 4 and 5.

Hold the cards and coins as illustrated in No. 6 and rub the back of the hand with the right forefinger; then let the hidden coin drop on the table.

Repeat the above instructions until all four coins are on the table.

This astonishing sleight-of-hand production is a wonderful introduction for the Coins of Sympathy.

CATCH IT   DROP IT

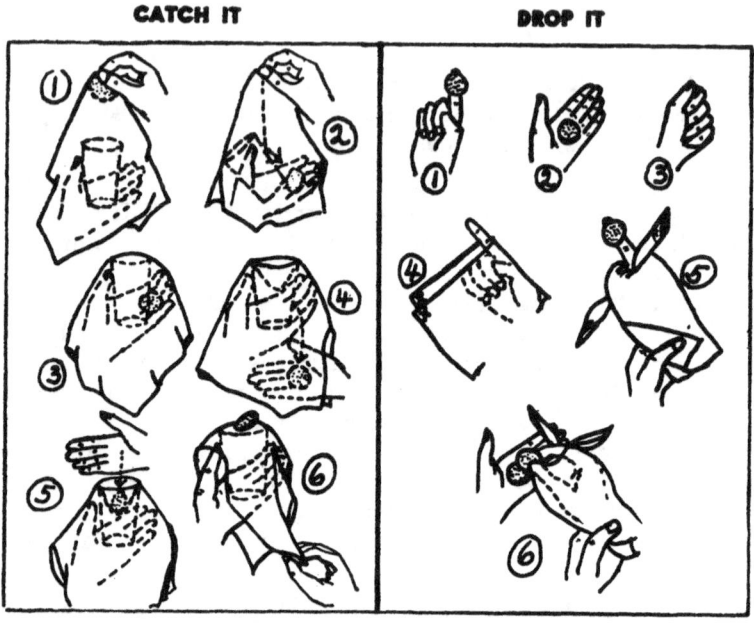

CATCH IT

REMARKS: the seemingly fairness of the performer in using articles at hand, and the enchantment given to it by the necessary primary preparations, make this one of the finest impromptu tricks ever invented. No difficult sleights are involved; only a requisite amount of caution is demanded.

EFFECT: A coin, which is in the bottom of a covered glass, is made to pass up through the exact center of the napkin.

DROP IT

REMARKS: You will find there are occasions when it is desirable, for personal reasons to single out a certain individual, in your circle of spectators. It is one of those rare effects that will allow you to corner a man; it may be that you wish to approach him later on a business deal; he may be a celebrity and you wish to have your photograph taken with him, and the beauty of the trick is, it can be done with spectators all around you.

EFFECT: A spectator holds a half dollar in the palm of his hand, and you balance another on the tip of your forefinger; the object is for you to bring the coin down against his and bring it back to its original position; the spectator is to close his hand when the coin strikes, to try and prevent you.

CATCH IT

HERE'S HOW: Under cover of a napkin, hold a half dollar over a glass and apparently drop the coin to the bottom; instead it strikes the tilted side where it falls into the left hand, as in Nos. 1 and 2.

Drape the napkin over the glass and invite a spectator to form a well by pushing the cloth into the glass. While he is doing so, secretly drop the coin into the right hand where it is palmed, as in No. 4.

You now claim you can make the coin in the bottom of the glass pass up through the cloth. So saying, the right hand illustrates with action, secretly dropping the coin into the well when you say "BOTTOM," and raising itself when you say "UP;" see No. 5.

Grasp the corner of the napkin as in No. 6 and slowly pull. This causes the coin to rise into view; continue to pull until the napkin is free of the glass and the coin will drop to the bottom.

You may find it to your advantage to use a duplicate coin which you hide in your right hand throughout the first part of the effect.

DROP IT

HERE'S HOW: Place a coin on your right forefinger and another in a spectator's palm, as in Nos. 1 and 2. Now say, "If I bring my coin down on yours, and if you close your hand quickly you will get both coins" (spectator's closed hand in No. 3). You do this several times, and please notice that the right thumb goes under the fingers; see No. 4; make sure that the spectators notice it also.

Tie a napkin around your hand, as illustrated in Nos. 4 and 5, and as soon as it is tied, get your thumb from under the fingers so as to be in readiness, then place one of the coins back on the forefinger; the other one is in the spectator's palm.

Once again you ask him to catch the coin, only this time, at the completion of the move, the coin is seen resting on your forefinger.

This is accomplished in transit by the right thumb and forefinger secretly holding the coin while it strikes; this action is hidden by the napkin; see No. 6.

This may be repeated several times, and at the conclusion of this splendid trick, get the thumb back under the fingers so that when the napkin is removed, no suspicion can be directed towards the guilty digit.

PRELUDE

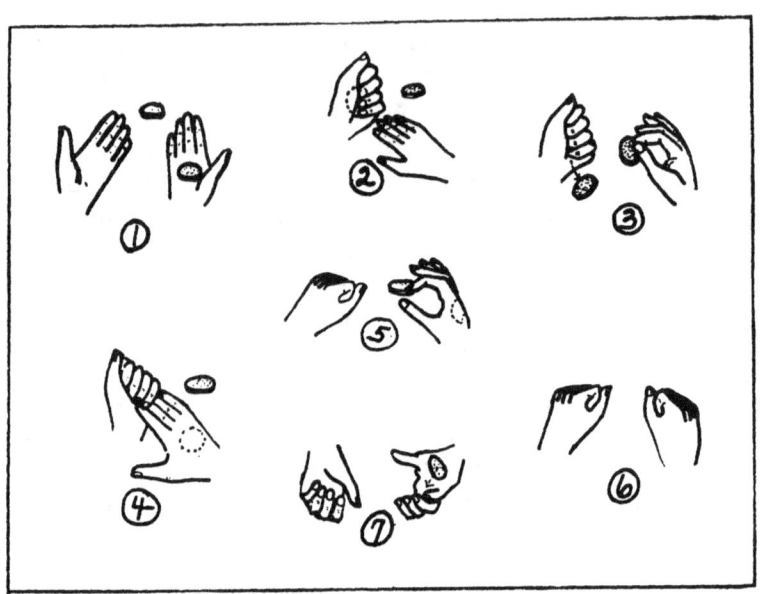

PRELUDE

REMARKS: Some performers make the mistake of opening their routine with a very difficult sleight-of-hand effect that requires the utmost confidence and manipulative ability to put it over.

This is wrong, for several reasons. If the trick should fail, it may cause a feeling of depression or nervousness to the now embarrassed performer, and a feeling of perplexity on the part of the suffering audience.

Neither the performer or the audience are keyed up enough at the start of the performance to warrant taking a chance of failing in the first trick. Under most circumstances, it is best to select some quick, easy trick that will not only get the atten-tion of the audience, but will at the same time, at its successful conclusion, give the performer a certain amount of confidence that is necessary for an exhibition in public. It will also serve to help banish whatever nervousness that may exist.

The above information is as much a secret as any item in this book, and we suggest that you try the following trick for a perfect opening. It is easy to perform, and has the appear-ance of a startling sleight-of-hand trick; it contains just enough zest to get the performer percolating.

EFFECT: The performer holds a coin in each hand, and secretly makes one coin travel over to the other hand.

PRELUDE

HERE'S HOW: Two coins are used; one is in the right palm, while the other is lying on the table top, as in No. 1.

Drop the coin into the left hand, as in No. 2. Now pick up the coin from the table and while doing so, let the left hand coin fall from the fist as if it were an accident; see No. 3.

Once again hold the coin as in No. 1, with the second coin lying on the table top as before, and with the very same move employed before, make a "PASS" by apparently placing the coin in the left hand, only this time the coin is retained by palming; see No. 4.

Holding both hands as in No. 5, pick the coin up from the table, and both hands go into a fist while you tell the spectators what you intend to do, and that is to make one coin go over to the other hand without their seeing how it was done; before anyone can challenge you to open each fist, you raise your fist from the table top, as in No. 7, and let the top coin drop down on the other.

NOTE: The "PASS" used for this trick and described above has been selected as one of the few natural "PASSES;" it contains no hand waving, but a perfect natural movement. Unfortunately, some performers kill a good trick by giving it the kiss of death with unusual positions of the hands.

A DOUBLE PASS   WAX IT

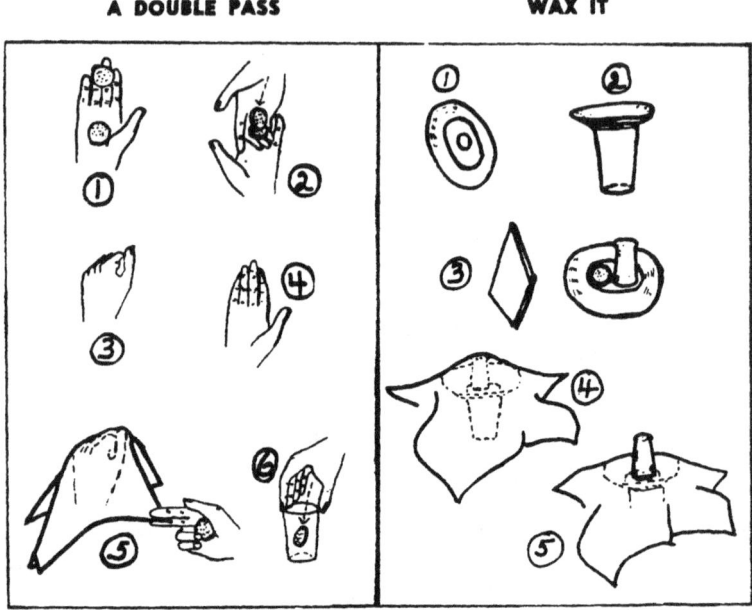

A DOUBLE PASS

REMARKS: This is a good follow-up from the proceeding one, and it is not a repetition, so you are free to perform it without the feeling you have violated one of the first rules of magic.

EFFECT: Two coins are made to secretly pass over to an empty glass.

WAX IT

REMARKS: Every Magician who has reached the point of accomplishment, has his own version of this famous trick, and there are many ways. In this version we resort to the use of wax; there are, of course, dozens of ways to do this with sleight-of-hand, so don't feel badly about cheating. If our stage illusionists have trap doors, wires, mirrors, and a half dozen assistants helping to vanish a rabbit, then it is in order for you to cheat also.

EFFECT: A half dollar is placed in a saucer and it is set upon a glass, then covered with a napkin; at the command of the performer, the coin is heard to drop down into the glass.

A DOUBLE PASS

HERE'S HOW: Hold two half dollars in the right hand in the position illustrated in No. 1. Now make a "PASS" by pretending to place the two coins into the left hand; in No. 2. Notice how the upper coin falls down on the lower one to cause a click, the left hand closing as if receiving the coins, as in No. 3, while the right hand back palms the two coins, as in No. 4.

In the act of reaching for a napkin, the two coins are shifted back to the front of the hand where they are palmed, while you spread the napkin over the left hand, as in No. 5.

Pick up a glass, as in No. 6, and pretend to make the coins pass up the left sleeve, across the chest, then down the right sleeve to the glass, letting one coin drop at a time.

WAX IT

HERE'S HOW: Secretly stick a small dab of wax or chewing gum on the bottom of a saucer, as in No. 1, then place a half dollar on the wax; also stick another dab of wax on the bottom of a salt shaker.

When you are ready to present the trick, set the saucer on a glass and into the saucer drop a duplicate half dollar; then place the shaker in the saucer, as illustrated in No. 3.

Announce that you will make the coin go through the saucer. You set the shaker on the coin "to give it weight," so you say; you continue by saying "I will also cover the setup so that you cannot see how the penetration takes place." See No. 4.

Now, using any excuse that may occur, you reach under the napkin and remove the shaker which has the coin sticking to the bottom and place it on top of the napkin, as in No. 5. You must exercise some care so that the coin will not be seen; you may even have an opportunity to scrape it off into your lap.

Move the saucer around so that the edge of the glass will dislodge the coin, causing it to fall into the glass, remove the napkin and show the coin in the bottom.

CHANGE IT   **SALT & PEPPER**

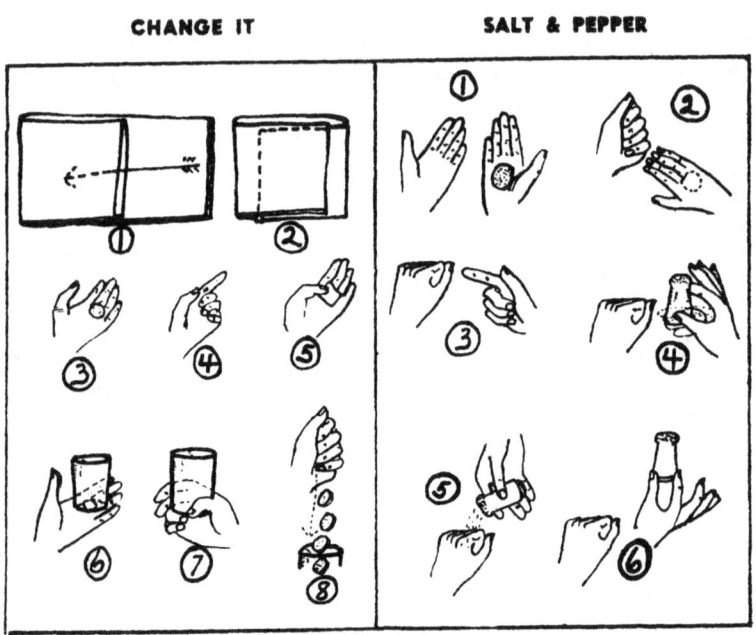

CHANGE IT

REMARKS: This trick is one of those gems that Magicians are always on the lookout for. It is very easy to do, and it is well received by the audience.

EFFECT: The Magician in a mysterious presentation changes four quarters to a dollar bill.

SALT AND PEPPER

REMARKS: This routine is one of the hardest to perform without detection. To be successful, it must be presented with a good deal of showmanship. Professional Magicians who perform from table to table in a nite club will like this offering.

EFFECT: The performer "PASSES" a coin under a salt shaker.

CHANGE IT

HERE'S HOW: Hide four quarters at the base of the fingers; see Nos. 3 and 4. Now practice folding a dollar bill as in Nos. 1 and 2, while holding the coins. Please notice that the bill, when folded, interlocks; this prevents it from unfolding at an inopportune moment.

After you have succeeded in mastering the above instructions with the bill, you are ready to proceed with the presentation. Now hold the bill with the right finger tips while the left hand, which is hiding the four quarters, pulls up the left sleeve; then the bill is laid down on top of the four quarters, as in No. 5, while the right hand pulls up the left sleeve.

On top of the bill you set a glass which has a bit of sticky substance on the bottom. You may try wetting the bottom, but after a few trials you will be convinced that it is best to be sure that the bill will stick. For this reason we suggest that you use some sticky substance, or you may have a dab of wax on the bill at a certain spot, so that when the bill is folded, the glass will set down on it. See No. 6.

The right hand now makes a few mysterious circular movements over the glass, and then lifts up the glass away from the left hand; the left hand goes into a fist to hide the quarters from sight. You close the routine by dropping the quarters into the glass. See Nos. 7 and 8.

SALT AND PEPPER

HERE'S HOW: Proceed to make a "PASS," as in Nos. 1, 2 and 3. Pick up the shaker, as in No. 4. Notice that the fingers are spread out; now in carrying the shaker back towards the body, the fingers curl under the palm so that the coin can be dropped upon them; now straighten out the fingers and set the shaker down on top of the coin; see No. 5. You must practice so you can set the shaker down on the coin without any noise. In performing at the dinner table, there may be enough noise in the room to muffle the slight sound you may make.

You must have an excuse for picking up the shaker, so call it magic powder and sprinkle some on the left fist; this move will give you the opportunity to adjust the coin so that you will be able to set the shaker back on the table, as in No. 6.

Make a throwing motion towards the shaker and lift it up, exposing the coin.

The sleight-of-hand expert will, of course, make use of both shakers. After he loads the first one, he will make use of a "PASS" known as "PUSH-IN-THE-FIST PASS" with a second coin, then slipping this coin under the other shaker.

COPPER & SILVER   **WATCH IT**

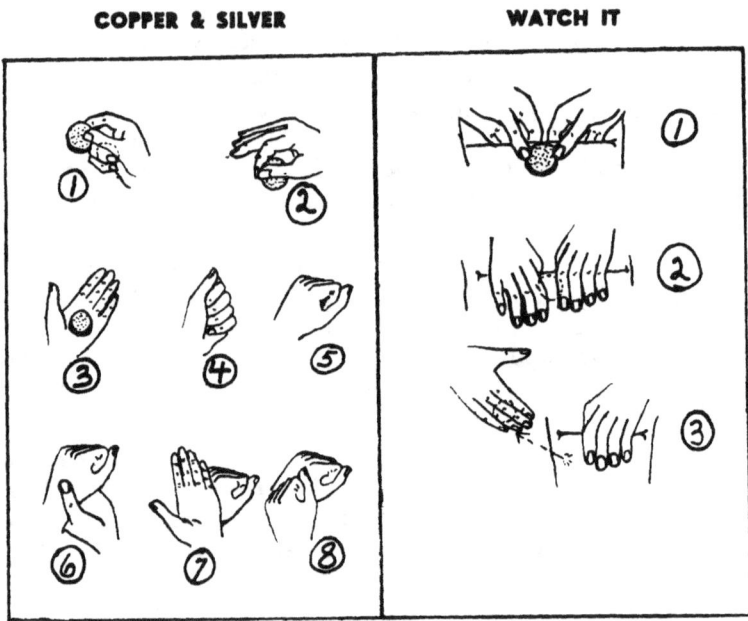

COPPER & SILVER

REMARKS: This routine demands of the performer considerable address almost to the point of officiousness. You are dealing with another person in whose hand you place a coin, and he must do exactly as you say, otherwise you will fail.

EFFECT: A copper and a silver coin change places.

WATCH IT

REMARKS: Here is a trick that is a favorite with many Magicians. There are many versions; the above is the one that has the most effect on the spectators.

EFFECT: A coin goes through the cloth of the trousers into the pocket.

COPPER & SILVER

HERE'S HOW: On the table top place a half dollar and an English penny. In the right hand have a duplicate half dollar palmed.

Pick up the penny from the table and curl the fingers against the hidden half, as in No. 1. Invite a spectator to hold out his hand; now slap the penny down into his palm, telling him to close his hand into a fist and then to turn his hand over, as in Nos. 4 and 5, your left hand assisting and directing, as in No. 6.

You now tell your victim that he is not closing his hand quickly enough; you repeat the above several times so he instantly turns his hand over into a fist when the coin strikes.

You are now prepared to make the switch; once again you ask the spectator to catch the coin; this time, as the right hand descends, you open up the fingers, letting the hidden coin go to his palm instead of the penny; with the left hand turn his hand over, and palm the penny in the right hand.

Hold your hand on his fist, as in No. 7. Pick up the half from the table and in the act of placing it in your left hand, substitute it for the hidden penny.

Both hands are now shown and the two coins have apparently changed places.

WATCH IT

HERE'S HOW: When you reach into your pocket to bring out all the change that may be there, you ascertain if you have two coins alike; let us say there are two half dollars there, so while the hand is in the pocket push one of the halves up to the top of the pocket; now empty the pocket by turning it inside out and lay the change on the table; push the pocket back, letting the hidden coin drop down.

Pick up the other half from the table and gather a fold in the leg of the trousers; place the half directly over the hidden coin, as in No. 1.

Turn the fold over, as in No. 2, and draw the half towards the palm with the right thumb.

Now take away the right hand, as in No. 3, and remove the left hand with the exception of the left forefinger, which is held against the fold; invite someone to feel the coin through the cloth; they will, of course, feel the coin in the pocket and think it is the one that they saw you press against the cloth.

You now conclude by straightening out the fold and reaching into the pocket, removing the coin that is there.

THE COIN STAR   **THE COIN ROLL**

THE COIN STAR

REMARKS: The coin star is one of the most beautiful in the art of coin magic, but it is so seldom seen because it is so very difficult to master. With the method described here it is as easy as one, two, three.

EFFECT: Five coins are placed in the left fist and they find their way back to the tips of the right fingers.

THE COIN ROLL

REMARKS: Here is another flourish that is so seldom seen before an audience; in fact even the audience can't see it most of the time. That, perhaps, is why most professional Magicians shun the use of it before a large group.

The method described here will greatly help the audience to see the coin rolling across the fingers.

EFFECT: The performer causes a large size coin to roll across his fingers.

THE COIN STAR

HERE'S HOW: First practice with four coins by placing them on the finger tips, as in No. 1, then bring the fingers together, slightly tilting the hand, as in No. 2; now quickly turn the hand back to the No. 1 position. The momentum should carry the coins back safely.

After you have mastered this move, bring the coins down on the table top, as in No. 3, and back to No. 1. After you get this down perfectly, proceed by placing a small dab of wax or chewing gum on another coin and stick it on the thumb, as in No. 4.

You can now repeat the above moves and need not have any worries about the coin on the thumb; the wax will take care of it.

You are now ready to present your trick, so make a "PASS" with the five coins, as in No. 5. The left fist now rests on the table top, as in No. 6, while the right hand goes under the table, and while attention is on what you are saying, you get the coins back to the finger tips, slap the left hand down on the table and bring out the coins so that they will be as in No. 1.

THE COIN ROLL

HERE'S HOW: Hold a large size coin, as in No. 1. The left thumb pushes it over the back of the forefinger, as in Nos. 2 and 3; then the second finger lifts up and tilts it over to the back of its finger, and the third finger does the same; finally the little finger tilts it up so it will slide down between itself and the third finger, where it meets the thumb, which is under to receive it; the thumb drags it around against the roots of the fingers to the starting point, and you repeat the same move.

We include this age-old classic of magic so that you will be able to present it in such a manner that everyone in the audience can see what you are doing.

The correct way to hold the hand while the coin is rolling, is in No. 3, and not as in No. 4. The back of the fingers will serve as a background and will enable the audience to see the coin more clearly.

You may experience some difficulty in keeping the coin from dropping to the floor, but perseverance will bring its reward.

FOUR TO GO

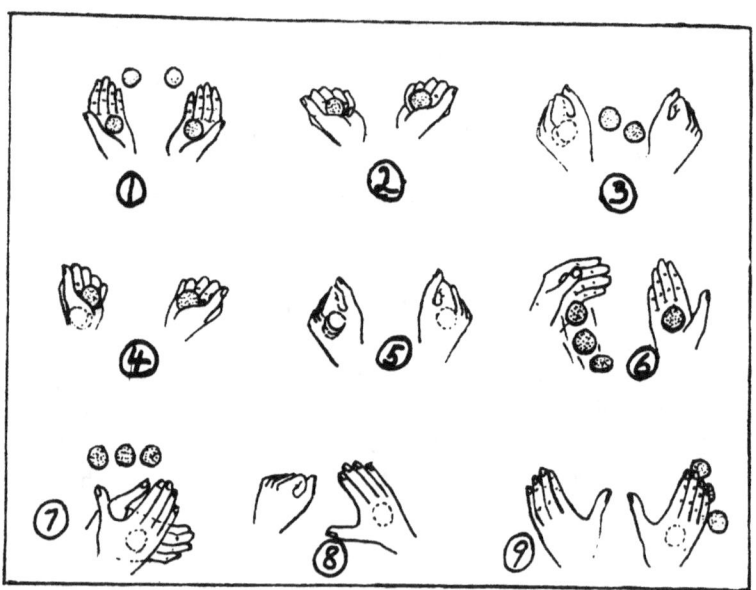

FOUR TO GO

REMARKS: This routine will live forever. More amateur Magicians use this routine than any other coin effect that I know of. There is no doubt that this is so because there are no sleights involved, and the effect is so great that the performer receives credit for a very brilliant display of dexterity. This trick has one weak spot in it that cannot be eliminated; it requires the performer to miss at the beginning of the routine, and that is unheard of for a top notch sleight-of-hand expert, hence many of our best men refrain from showing it. The point I am trying to put over is this, there will be some in the audience who will pay less attention after you have missed.

EFFECT: Two coins are in each fist; you now make the coins in one hand go over invisibly to the other hand.

FOUR TO GO

HERE'S HOW: Use four coins, place two on the table and two in the hands, as in No. 1.

Close the hands into a fist, and have a spectator place the two on the table on your hands, as in No. 2.

Hold both hands about 12 inches away and announce that you will make the coins travel together. Suddenly turn the hands over, and here comes the piece of business (the miss); the right hand drops both of its coins, while the left hand opens and closes so it will have two coins, as in No. 3. The spectators believe that you have a coin in each hand and the two on the table were the two that were resting on your fingers.

In an apologetic manner for your apparent failure, you ask a spectator to again place the coins from the table to your hands; see No. 4. Again you turn your hands over, letting the coins resting on your fingers drop into the fists, as in No. 5. Now open both hands, letting the left hand coins drop on the table, as illustrated in No. 6. Now make a "PASS" with the right hand coin, as in Nos. 7 and 8.

Bring down both hands flat on the table simultaneously, as in No. 9. The sound of the coin striking the table sounds as if it came from the left hand. To conclude, you command the coin to pass over.

FOLD IT

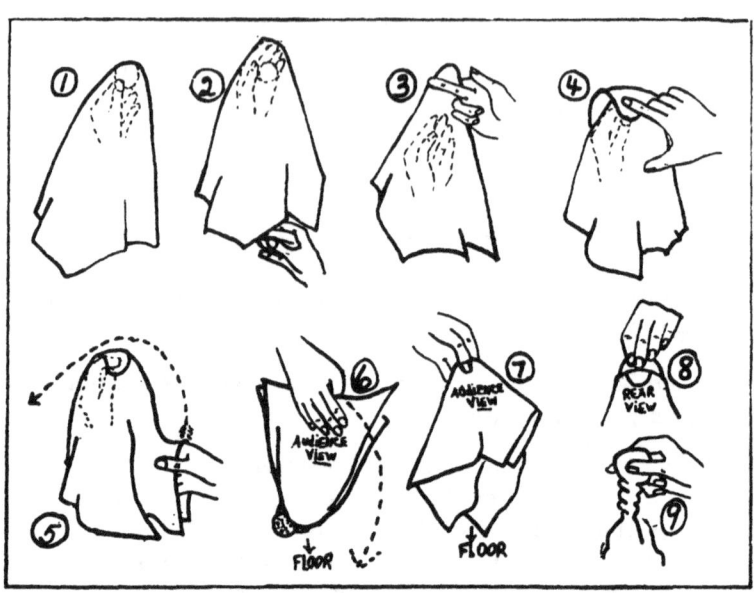

FOLD IT

REMARKS: No book on coin tricks would be complete without this classical napkin fold. Included will be a very fine table trick.

Most performers, when presenting this effect, fail to take advantage of a principle in magic described in the Magician's vernacular as a "Sucker move."

After a coin has been placed under a napkin, you lift up one side of the cloth to ostensibly prove the coin is still there, but actually it is done for the purpose of secretly getting the coin on the outside of the cloth, where it is hidden in one of the folds. The audience believes the coin is under the napkin.

It is our belief that a sucker move must be employed so that you will have a perfectly good reason for lifting up the cloth to prove the coin is still there. Time after time we have seen performers make this fold and, for no reason whatsoever, would say, "I'll turn the cloth over so you can see that the coin is still there." The audience should have no reason for not believing it isn't there unless you have led them to doubt it.

EFFECT: A penetration.

FOLD IT

HERE'S HOW: Hold a large size coin in the left hand and cover it, as in No. 1.

Now comes the sucker move. While pattering, let the right hand stray under the cloth and at the same time let the coin drop down from the left finger tips; immediately remove the right hand and hold it in such a way that it appears you are trying to hide something; see No. 2.

Some one is sure to call you on this, so you proceed as illustrated and show that the coin is still there.

The right hand should grasp the coin through the cloth; as in No. 3, and turn it over as in No. 4; the left fingers will now take hold of the coin; then withdraw the right hand away from the napkin.

The right hand will hold the edge of the napkin which is nearest the audience and bring it over the wrist, as in Nos. 5 and 6.

Please notice that, at this point, the coin points to the floor; now with the right thumb grasp the other edge of the napkin which should be lying across the wrist and bring both down, as directed by the arrow so it will appear as in No. 7. A rear view of the fold is illustrated in No. 8.

The above is the fold and there are many tricks that can be accomplished by it. A brief one will follow

Drape another napkin over the No. 8 setup, and twist both napkins together, as in No. 9; presently let them untwist themselves with the right hand holding, as in No. 9; the inside napkin will fall to the floor, and the coin appears to have penetrated it.

RED & BLUE

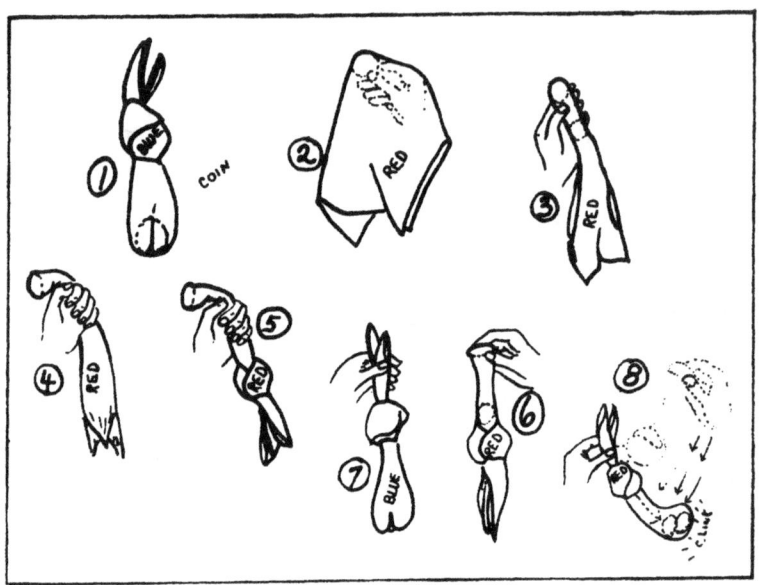

RED & BLUE

REMARKS: Here is another routine that is based partly on the fold described on page 21. We respectively present our version.

Previous to this we have been instructed to have two persons hold the two different napkins, each of which apparently covers one coin; this has always been the weak spot in the routine because of the unnatural position they assumed when holding the napkins. Sometimes they would feel the coin through the fake fold; again they would let one end drop and expose the fact that a duplicate coin was being used. Our claim is that we have eliminated this danger spot by simply tieing a knot in each napkin and having one person hold both, with one in each hand.

EFFECT: A coin travels from under one napkin to another.

RED & BLUE

HERE'S HOW: Use two large Bandannas, one red and the other blue. Make a fake fold over a coin in the blue cloth and tie a knot in it, as in No. 1. Your excuses for offering to tie the knot could be many; one being that you do not want the coin to fall to the floor; the real reason being that your helper can hold the cloth with one hand, as in No. 7.

The right hand has palmed another duplicate coin and holds at the finger tips still another duplicate coin. Drape the red cloth over the right hand, as in No. 2. The left hand now takes hold of the top coin through the cloth and the right hand is withdrawn, leaving the hidden coin at the spot indicated in illustration No. 3.

You may, if you wish, offer someone to feel the coin, as in No. 4; now tie a knot in it, as in No. 5. This knot will keep the hidden coin from falling out, and let the spectator hold the cloth with his other free hand, as in Nos. 6 and 7.

Announce to the spectator that you will make the coin in the blue cloth pass over to the red one; ask him if he wants it to go visibly or invisibly. Whatever answer he gives, you openly reach over and pull the coin out and make a "PASS"; now take hold of the red cloth with the hand that has the coin palmed, then make a throwing motion towards the red cloth with the left hand, which is supposed to have the coin; you now jerk the cloth out of his hand, as in No. 8. This will cause the upper coin to drop down on the lower one.

IN THE BAG

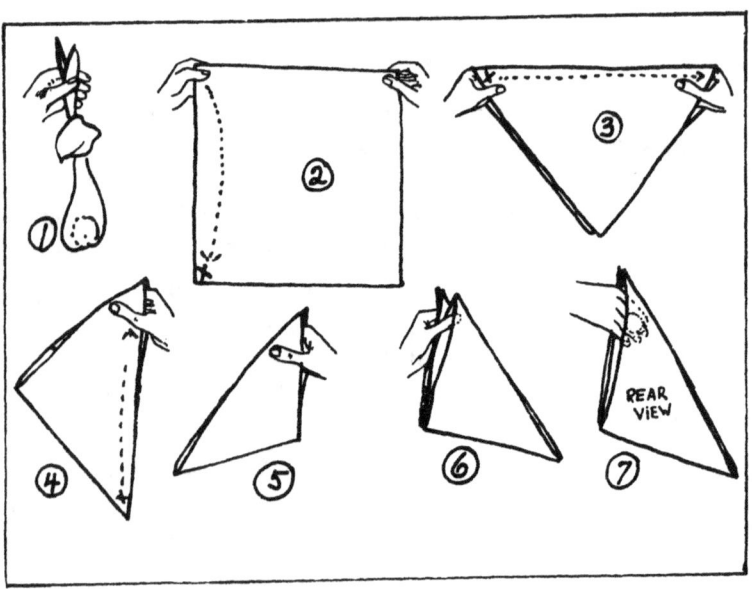

IN THE BAG

REMARKS: While on the subject of the fake fold, we give you still another routine that may be performed with it. As far as the audience is concerned, we believe this routine is one of the best ever offered to the public.

EFFECT: Four coins are tied up in a large kerchief; another large kerchief of a different color is formed into a bag; the four coins are then made to pass, invisibly, over to the bag.

IN THE BAG

HERE'S HOW: The napkin fold described on page 11 is used to hold the four coins; after placing them in and tieing up, as in No. 1, you request someone to hold them. The other kerchief is formed into the bag in this manner; first hold it up, as in No. 2; then the left hand holds the X corner so it will appear as in No. 3; next the X corner in No. 3 goes over to the right hand to form No. 4; finally the X corner in No. 4 goes up to the right hand to form No. 5. Pass the bag over to the left hand, as in No. 6, and please notice that the left thumb is under one of the folds; this is so that when the right hand desires to go into the now-formed bag it will form an opening.

With the right hand reach over to the blue kerchief and hold at the spot where the coins are; ask the spectator to pull on his end to make the knot tighter; while this is being done you secretly take away the four coins. The spectator now holds the bag by himself. If the kerchief is of a heavy material, the absence of the coins will not be noticed by the reduced weight. The right hand goes into the kerchief bag at the spot where the left thumb indicates in No. 6, and holds the bag as in No. 7; this is a rear view.

You now reach over to the blue kerchief and pretend to take away one coin and throw it into the bag, dropping one coin from the right hand, repeat until all coins are over.

THE TUBE

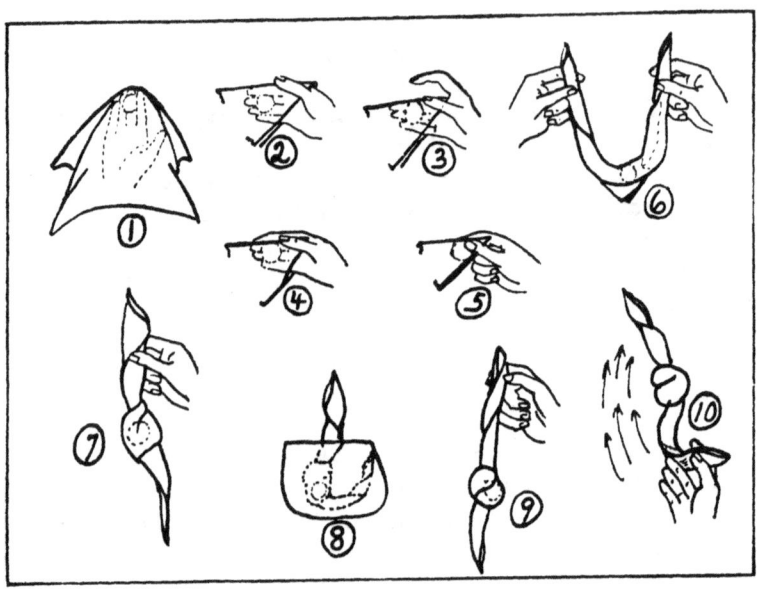

THE TUBE

REMARKS: This routine is included because we believe we have, after many years, developed a wonderful routine based on a simple move that will be described on the next page.

EFFECT: A napkin is tied into a knot, and a coin is made to pass invisibly to the inside of the knot.

THE TUBE

HERE'S HOW: Hide a half dollar in the right hand and cover it with a napkin; under cover of the cloth, get the coin in the position illustrated in No. 1. This may be done while you are inviting someone to look at the center of the napkin to be sure there are no holes in it.

Now make a tube in the napkin, so that the hidden coin will slide down. The right hand is partly withdrawn and holds one corner, while the left hand holds the opposite corner; the right hand should be as in No. 2.

Now withdraw the right forefinger, as in No. 3, then hold the coin through the cloth with the thumb and this forefinger as in No. 4; next take out the other three fingers and hold the coin and the cloth as in No. 5. Now give the napkin a twist or two and let the hidden coin drop down in the tube, as in No. 6.

Tie a knot in the napkin, as in No. 7, making sure the coin goes into the knot.

Place the napkin in the right side pocket with one end showing, as in No. 8.

Make a "PASS" with a duplicate coin and in reaching for the napkin, drop the coin into the pocket; this makes a perfect move for getting rid of the coin; bring out the napkin and hold it with the three fingers against the palm, as in No. 9.

Now make your throwing motion towards the cloth, at the same time moving the three lower right hand fingers quickly outwards against the napkin, causing it to jump up in the air, as in No. 10. It appears as though the coin struck the cloth.

COINS OF SYMPATHY

COINS OF SYMPATHY

REMARKS: May we suggest that when you present this routine, you first produce the coins as described on page 4.

EFFECT: Four coins lying some distance apart are made to mysteriously collect together.

COINS OF SYMPATHY

HERE'S HOW: Lay four coins on a napkin, as in No. 1. Hold a card in each hand and move the cards around the napkin, covering two coins at a time. After you have covered the coins several times, get the Two of Hearts over the upper right hand coin and pinch it against the back of the card; bring over the Three of Diamonds to partly cover it, and bring away the Two of Hearts with the hidden coin under it; at the same time lay the Three of Diamonds down; see No. 2. Place the Two of Hearts and the coin, as illustrated in No. 3.

You now pick up the lower left hand coin and pretend that you will place the coin under the napkin; the right hand travels under the cloth but deposits the coin in the left fingers; withdraw the right hand and bring back the Two of Hearts to show you now have two coins under the cloth. Apparently the coin under the cloth has passed through the napkin; see Nos. 4 and 5.

The Two of Hearts is laid on the left fingers, hiding the coin and the left fingers bring it up to the upper left hand corner; you repeat with the lower right hand corner coin, finally pretending to blow over the coin which is supposed to be under the Three of Diamonds.

CONCLUDING REMARKS

It goes without saying that before you present any of these effects before an audience, you must learn them thoroughly, and even then for the first few times after you have shown them, you should make several changes that will suit your personality.

I have no doubt that anyone can learn the tricks, but whether you are able to present them with a display of personality is another thing.

Simply speaking, a presentation with a display of your personality means putting your best foot forward.

www.ingramcontent.com/pod-product-compliance
Lightning Source LLC
Chambersburg PA
CBHW050905120626
46554CB00003B/1017